KIN OF CAIN

KIN OF CAIN
A Short Bernicia Tale

Matthew Harffy

First published in the UK in 2017 by Aria, an imprint of Head of Zeus Ltd

9 7 5 3 1 2 4 6 8

A CIP catalogue record for this book is available from the British Library.

ISBN 9781784978860

Aria
c/o Head of Zeus
First Floor East
5–8 Hardwick Street
London EC1R 4RG

www.ariafiction.com

For Alex, the best of friends and fellow traveller
through countless fantastic worlds.

Anno Domini Nostri Iesu Christi
In the Year of Our Lord
Jesus Christ
630

One

The scream silenced the mead hall like a slap to the face of a noisy child.

A chill ran through the throng. The brittle laughter died on lips that quickly twisted from smiles to scowls. The warm hubbub of moments before was shattered as easily as the thin skin of ice that formed on the puddles in the courtyard outside.

One of the hounds looked up from where it gnawed a bone by the hearth fire and whimpered.

Ælfhere, the scop, lowered his lyre, the last, interrupted notes, jangling in the air.

Octa set aside the mead horn he had been drinking from. His senses were dulled by the drink, but not enough that the small hairs on the back of his neck did not prickle with the sound of anguish that came from outside the hall. He turned to his friend, Bassus, who sat on his left. The huge warrior's brow furrowed. Bassus met his gaze and opened his mouth, but before he could speak, another scream rent the chill night that smothered the great hall.

There were words in that scream.

"The night-walker! The sceadugenga brings death!"

Night-walker. Shadow-goer.

Octa felt bony fingers of terror scratch down his spine. He shuddered, hoping none of the other king's warriors would notice. He had not long before joined the king's gesithas and some of the men were wary of him, he knew.

They had feasted; eating, drinking and boasting. Trying to ignore the one who haunted the dark winter paths. They had prayed, some to the old gods, others to the king's new Christ god, in the hope that the night devil would prove to be nothing more than a wild animal. A man could hunt an animal. Arrows would pierce a wolf or a bear's flesh. But deep down they had all been expecting more screams in the night. More death stalking the shadows. Few of those in the hall had seen the remains of the people who had been slain by the beast, but the tales of the corpses, ripped and raw, bones smashed, limbs removed, had reached them all. This was not the work of any animal. This was something else.

Something evil.

At the head of the hall, the imposing figure of the king surged to his feet. Edwin, King of Deira and Bernicia, pointed to the end of the hall where the door wardens stood.

"Open the doors," he said, his tone commanding.

The shorter of the two warriors who guarded the door hesitated. There was a murmur in the great hall. There were many present who did not wish to see the stout wooden doors opened to the night. For who knew what horrors dwelt there in the darkness?

"Lord?"

"You heard my words clearly," Edwin said. "Open the doors."

Another scream, closer now.

"I am king of the folk of these lands. I will not leave them outside in the dark while we feast in the fire-glow and warmth of my hall. Now, open the doors."

"Wait, lord king," Bassus' rumbling voice stilled the door ward's hand before he had lifted the bar. Edwin looked to his champion, arching an eyebrow at the interruption.

"You are right, of course," said Bassus, "but let us arm ourselves first. We know nothing of what awaits us beyond the walls of Gefrin's hall."

Edwin nodded. The door wards quickly distributed the weapons that had been left in their care. A hall crammed with drunken warriors carrying swords and seaxes was not wise, hence the precaution, but now protection of the king and the hall was more important.

Octa retrieved his seax. The weapon had been a gift from his uncle Selwyn and the smooth antler handle was comforting. For an instant his mind was filled with memories of his home in Cantware. Edita and Rheda. His mother. Beobrand. Would he ever see them again? As usual when he thought of them, he felt a pang of regret, a twist of guilt at having abandoned them. But Bernicia was his home now. Edwin his king, and the men around him, his sword-brothers.

He readied himself with the rest of the men near the doors of the great hall of Gefrin. Women and children huddled at the far end of the room, with the priests and the queen.

The reek of fear-sweat filled the air as another wail came from just outside.

"Open the doors!" roared Edwin.

The door wardens lifted the bar and swung the doors open.

Cold night air cut into the hall's muggy warmth like an icicle plunged into pliant flesh.

For a moment, nobody breathed. The hall was silent, all eyes staring into the utter blackness of the night.

Then, stepping out of the dark and into the frame of the doorway, came a vision from nightmare. Blood-slick and steaming, staggered a figure into the hall. The men stepped back, without thinking, wishing to be distanced from this ghoul. The women gasped. The dark-robed priest, Paulinus, raised the amulet he wore at his neck and recited words of magic in the secret tongue of the Christ followers.

The figure's eyes were bright in the mask of gore he wore. His mouth opened. Yet no otherworldly screech issued forth, instead words tumbled, quick and desperate.

"Help me. Help me. The nihtgenga came. It killed them. Killed them all." Babbling as it came, the figure stumbled.

This was no night-stalker. No creature of evil. This was a man.

Octa was the first to react. He leapt forward, catching the poor wretch before he could fall to the rush-strewn floor. He was as cold as the bones of the dead, sticky to the touch with the slaughter-dew that covered him. And he trembled like a child with a fever.

"Quick," said Octa, his voice snapping the watching thegns into action, "a stool here, by the fire. This man is near to frozen. We need warm water too." Octa's tone demanded to be heeded, and yet there was a momentary pause. This young man from Cantware did not lead here. The people

4

looked to their leader. King Edwin assented with his head and the hall burst once more into life.

Soon the man was seated beside the hearth. A thrall had brought a bowl of water and worked the worst of the cloying blood from the man's features. In his hand he now held a cup of mead. The liquid spilt into his beard as he drank, such was his shaking. Drops of amber clung to the matted hair.

The doors had been closed and barred once more, but the hall was still quiet. They waited until he had drained the cup, but the atmosphere in the hall was as taut as a bowstring.

Edwin stepped forward, nodding to Octa as he passed. In his hands he held a bearskin. He made to drape the fur over the man, who still shook terribly. The man recoiled as if burnt, shying from the king.

"Easy now," said Edwin, his voice soothing, as one who addresses a scared animal. "I am your king. I mean you no harm. This is the skin of a great bear that I killed years ago. It will warm you." Edwin saw something in the man's expression. Understanding dawned. "This bear is long dead. Killed by my own hand. It was a fell beast, but it can harm no-one now. It cannot hurt you."

The man's eyes focused and he reached out a hand, tentatively caressing the fur. Edwin gently draped the skin over the man's shoulders and sat down facing him.

The king's retinue, his comitatus, crowded closer, to better hear what was said. Edwin gave them a stern stare. They took a pace back.

A log cracked in the fire, shifting into the embers and sending sparks spiralling towards the smoke-stained rafters.

The man started at the noise. He was not the only one to do so.

"I have told you my name," said Edwin, his voice still soft. "What is yours?"

The man looked lost for a moment. His eyes flicked around the watchers. The king waited patiently. At last the man spoke.

"I am Banstan, son of Banstan."

"Well come to the great hall of Gefrin, Banstan. Now, tell me what happened to you."

Banstan swallowed hard, looking down to his empty cup. The king took an earthenware pitcher from the table and poured more mead. Banstan took a long draught, then let out a shuddering sigh.

"It came upon us out of nowhere. Silent it was, until the killing started. We were bringing the sheep in, Breca and me." Banstan's face crumpled and tears began to fall. "Breca…" he said, in a hollow voice.

Something in Banstan's anguish spoke to Edwin.

"Your son?" he asked.

Banstan nodded. He let out a sobbing cry, pulling the bearskin around him and rocking forward and back.

"What happened? What was it that came upon you?"

"It was a giant. It came fast on two legs, like a man, but this was no man. Before we knew it, it had ripped the head from one of the sheep, as easy as pulling an ear of barley from a stalk. Breca was faster than me, he's a strong boy…" His words caught in his throat.

"Your son was brave, yes? What did he do?"

"Yes, brave and strong," continued Banstan, his pride in his boy giving his voice strength. "He ran at the thing with his spear, but it did no harm to it."

"No harm?"

"The blade was good iron, strong and sharp, but it bounced from the hide of the creature, as if its skin were made of stone. The nihtgenga laughed then."

"It laughed?" The hall was still and the fire did nothing to warm those who listened to the gruesome tale.

"A horrible sound... like boulders rubbing together... It laughed as it..." Banstan's words cracked. Tears flowed freely down his cheeks.

"What?" asked Edwin.

Paulinus stepped close to the king and spoke quietly in his unusual voice. He had come from over the sea, from a land far to the south where the Christ's followers ruled.

"Lord, this man has seen terrible things. He must be allowed to rest now."

Edwin gave Paulinus a withering look.

"This man will tell us all he has seen before he rests, Paulinus. Speaking the words will cause him no further harm, but I would know what has been attacking my people."

The tall priest nodded and retreated. He did not yet have the full support of the king, but Edwin turned to him more and more frequently for counsel.

"Speak, man," said Edwin, an edge of iron entering his voice, "tell us what happened, so that I may kill this beast."

"Nobody can slay this creature," said Banstan. His words were as empty as a winter forest. "It laughed as it ripped Breca's gut-ropes from his stomach. It laughed as I ran at it. I turned and I looked into its face a moment before..."

"Before?"

Banstan took a deep breath. "It must have hit me, for the next thing I remember was waking to hear the crunch and slaver of the monster eating. It was feasting on my son's body like a lord eating a roast boar. I was behind it then. I should have tried to kill it. To avenge my son. But, Woden help me, I knew I could not cut it, so I turned and fled into the night."

There was silence in the hall. Octa felt for Banstan. He had not only lost his son, but now he was shamed before the king and his thegns.

Edwin spoke the words Octa was thinking.

"But if you had stayed to fight, Banstan, you would not have been able to tell your king of what you had seen. Breca's death would have been in vain if you too had been slain."

Banstan sat up slightly straighter on the stool.

"Are you quite sure if was not a bear?" asked Edwin.

"Aye. It was no bear."

"And not a man."

"Not a man, lord. This was no mortal thing. It is a nihtgenga, a night-stalker. A monster from the otherworld and nothing can slay it."

Edwin placed a hand on Banstan's shoulder for a moment, then stood abruptly.

"Well, we'll have to see about that," he said.

Two

"It is the son of Cain," hissed Paulinus.

Edwin, Paulinus, Bassus and several of the king's most trusted thegns were gathered at the end of the hall. It was late. The shapes of slumbering men, women and children were dotted throughout the hall. Banstan had eventually fallen into a troubled sleep. Once the hall was quiet, the king had called this small group together to discuss what should be done about this nihtgenga that harried the land. Octa was surprised and pleased to be included. He sensed the eyes of envious warriors on him as Bassus roused him from where he lay to join the king.

"Cain?" asked Octa.

Paulinus seemed annoyed at the question from the young man, but then, perhaps realising this gave him a chance to talk of the holy book of the Christ, he relaxed and said, "Cain, son of Adam, was the first murderer. A kin slayer. He slew his brother Abel and was thus accursed by the Lord to never know peace. The land refused to yield up its bounty to Cain after it had tasted his brother Abel's blood. Cain's offspring are evil giants. Unquiet spirits who roam the night and feast on the flesh of man."

Octa shuddered. Did the priest seem to be enjoying this?

"Is it true that no blade can hurt it?" Edwin asked.

"I do not know," said Paulinus.

"So far, this thing has killed women and boys," Bassus growled. "Shepherds, thralls, ceorls. We shall see how it fares against a warrior."

The men hoomed in the back of their throats. Bassus was huge and skilled in the arts of battle. It would take a lot to kill him.

"I cannot have this thing harm more of my people. I took Bernicia and Deira from Æthelfrith and promised the people – my people – protection. If they are unsafe, I am not a good king."

The image of his father, Grimgundi, came into Octa's mind then. His mother, sisters and younger brother cowering from the brute. Should he have stayed in Cantware to protect them from Grimgundi? He had known that he had to get away. His thoughts had turned dark, and he was no kin slayer. No kith of Cain.

"I will seek out this monster and slay him," Octa said into the silence of the hall, his voice travelling beyond the small group of men, to those who lay feigning sleep.

"Will you, young Octa?" Edwin's teeth flashed bright in the gloom. "Perhaps you will at that. But I will not send you alone. I would be sure that we are rid of this menace once and for all. Bassus, you will go with Octa."

"Of course, my lord."

"And Wiglaf, Gram and Unferth. Five of my finest warriors should be enough to slay this beast. Now, sleep, for at first light you set forth to find this creature, this nihtgenga, this kin of Cain. And when you find it, you are to let it know that Edwin, son of Aella, King of Bernicia and Deira will not suffer it to live within his lands. Find this thing and bring me back its head."

As they picked their way back to their spaces on the crowded floor, Bassus clapped Octa on the shoulder.

"I'm glad Edwin invited me along. I wouldn't want you to have all the fun."

Octa didn't reply. He could hear the smile in Bassus' words, but he felt no mirth.

Octa wrapped himself in his cloak and listened to the creak of the timbers of the hall. He wondered at his words to the king. What had prompted him to speak up so?

Somewhere, out there in the night, stalked a creature that had ripped a young man apart before eating him like so much meat. What if Banstan had spoken true? What if no blade could harm it? But it was as Edwin had said, the people must be protected by their king, and Octa was one of Edwin's gesithas. It was his wyrd to serve his lord. To defend the king and his people.

At last sleep came. Octa's dreams were haunted by visions of a giant beast with the fur of a bear. It had its back to Octa. Its dark bulk was hunched over a corpse. It was feeding, the crack of bones and the slimy sounds of sucking were loud in the still night air. Octa ran towards the beast, pulling his seax from its scabbard.

As he came close enough to strike, moonlight fell on the face of the cadaver that the monster was feasting upon. It was Octa's brother, Beobrand.

Aghast, Octa swung his blade at the creature. The seax made contact, but it was as if he had struck stone. The seax clanged against the hide of the beast, but did no harm.

The nihtgenga, shaggy and huge, raised itself up to its full, monstrous height and began to laugh. The sound of that laughter terrified Octa. It was not the sound of boulders crashing together that Banstan had spoken of.

It was the sound of his father.

Three

The morning was crisp, the sky bright and pale over the hills surrounding Gefrin. The valley and the hall were still in shadow when they left. Edwin had provided his thegns with fine horses from his stables. Banstan, as pallid as the frost-licked grass of the hills, walked before them. He had been commanded to lead them to where the beast had attacked. He trembled and shook as he walked and Octa noticed the shepherd brushing tears from his cheeks when he believed nobody was watching. Banstan was a broken man, but he had straightened his back at Edwin's order and nodded. He would not again turn away from his duty.

At Banstan's side padded a scrawny, tan-and-white sheepdog. It too seemed crestfallen, ears down, tail low, as if it regretted not being able to defend its master's son from the beast that had attacked in the dark. Where it had been when Banstan came to the hall, Octa did not know. Perhaps it had fled and only returned in the light of day. But like its master, though scared, the animal looked determined to do what was required of it.

As they made their way towards the rising sun, Octa glanced back at the great hall of Gefrin. Beyond the hall, with its painted doors and glistening shingle roof stood the wooden bones of a new structure. A strange building that Paulinus had begged the king to allow him to build. It was not yet finished, but Octa believed it would be somewhere for the priest to address many men on raised platforms. He shrugged. The ways of priests were strange. Reaching to his side, he once again checked that his seax was in its sheath.

None of the other riders seemed to show any fear, which only served to make Octa all the more acutely aware of his own anxiety.

At the front of the group rode Bassus, the king's champion. He was huge, skilled in combat and seemingly frightened of nothing. He wore a byrnie of iron and a great woollen cloak, trimmed with fur. A fine sword hung from his belt. Octa liked him. The older warrior had treated him like a younger brother ever since Octa had arrived in Bernicia. They practised the use of blade, spear and shield together. Bassus was a good teacher and Octa had quickly grown in battle-skill.

Next to Bassus was his close friend, Gram. Gram was almost as tall as Bassus, but slimmer. As straight as a spear, was how Bassus had described him to Octa. He had not merely been referring to his stature and bearing. Gram was loyal and direct. Quick to laugh, yet cunning in battle. A formidable warrior.

Young Wiglaf sat astride a brown mare. Wiglaf was a quiet one. Smaller in stature than the others, and yet there was a solidity about him that Octa liked. Wiglaf never seemed to move quickly, but he was not slow. His eyes, fast and inquisitive, like silver fish darting beneath a frozen lake, spoke of a rapid wit.

Unferth was the oldest of the thegns. He carried a great sword at his side. Warrior rings adorned his arms. His byrnie and helm were polished and caught the morning sunlight. He had seldom spoken to Octa before. He rarely smiled, treated the younger warriors with contempt and never uttered a pleasant word. Unferth's hair, perhaps once thick and long, was now thin and streaked with grey. His war gear and rings attested to his prowess in battle, but that was not enough to make Octa like the man.

Perhaps sensing Octa's gaze, Unferth turned in his saddle to frown at him.

Octa's face grew hot, despite the chill morning air. He spurred his mount forward, towards Bassus and friendlier companions.

Banstan turned at his approach, terror pulling at his features. Octa chose to ignore the man's fear. To mention it would only shame him further.

"How far until we reach the place?" Octa asked.

Banstan swallowed and pointed to the east.

"Not long, lord," he said, the tremor in his voice unmistakable. "We graze the sheep over that ridge. The gods alone know how many that creature took. And if not him, the wolves will have got to them. We'll starve now. That's for sure."

He lowered his head and trudged on, brushing at his face with the heel of his hand.

Life was harsh. Octa had no idea how many mouths Banstan had waiting for him back at Gefrin, but to lose livestock would be devastating. He wondered whether the man and his family would need to place their heads in Edwin's hands before the winter was over. The shepherd had lost so much, Octa hoped he would not need to accept such a further blow to his pride. Of course, it could be that Banstan would manage, he thought grimly, with one less mouth to feed.

They crested the hill. The sun, still low in the sky, shone brightly on their faces. Octa squinted.

Scrubby grass, heather and bracken covered a long slope that ended in a dark wood of aspen and ash. Beyond that, Octa knew, lay more hills and forests before turning to marshland and then the sea. Mist still clung to the edge of the woods and in the deeper valleys. Off to the left and some way down the hillside seven or eight shaggy sheep cropped at the grass. A path of trampled grass and worn earth led down the slope. There was movement on the path, before it reached the trees. A dark shape writhed and fluttered there, surrounded by smaller shapes that heaved and pulsated.

Octa trembled and reached for his seax. What evil was this? Was the nihtgenga there still, gorging itself on the flesh of its victim?

Banstan let out a cry. His dog growled, its hackles raised.

Wiglaf kicked his horse into a canter and rode towards the dark forms on the path. As he approached Wiglaf yelled.

"Hey! Hey!"

What was he doing? He was brave, or moonstruck. But he too was one of Edwin's gesithas; one of Octa's shield-brothers. And Octa could not leave him to stand alone against the evil that lurked there.

He spurred his own steed forward. A moment later he understood what he had seen from the hilltop. There was no night-goer here. Was the sun not in the sky? There was no gloom for a shadow-stalker to hide in. Unless it stared at them from the shelter of the forest...

The moving lumps on the earth were the remains of the creature's feast.

At Wiglaf's shouts, flocks of carrion crows flapped angrily into the sky. They screeched their displeasure at having their own banquet interrupted. Some could barely fly, so engorged with food were they. They hopped away from the riders, cawing beaks red, wings as black as a winter's night.

Wiglaf dismounted. And bent to examine what the birds had left.

Octa reined in and slid from the saddle. The horse shied at the smell of the blood and he had to grip the reins tightly to avoid losing his mount.

Stepping forward, his stomach churned. His mouth filled with liquid. He breathed shallowly, willing himself not to puke.

Bassus, Gram and Unferth trotted up, but none dismounted. Behind them, Banstan began to keen and moan.

"Breca," he sobbed, running forward.

Bassus took one glance at the grisly piles of flesh and bone and turned his horse towards the shepherd.

"Banstan, do not approach," he said, his words clipped, his tone commanding. "Go, fetch your sheep yonder."

Banstan took a couple more tottering steps towards the gathered warriors.

"But, Breca... my boy..." he whimpered.

"You can do nothing now for him." Bassus' voice softened. "Think of your family. They'll be needing you to bring back those sheep if you are to survive the winter." Banstan looked up at the mounted thegn, eyes wide, tears streaming down his dirt-streaked cheeks. "Do as I say, Banstan, son of Banstan. We will see to your son."

Banstan drew in a shuddering breath and staggered away, towards his sheep. He let out a piercing whistle, and his dog raced towards the small flock of sheep.

"Well?" Bassus enquired of Wiglaf and Octa.

"It is as the man told us in the hall," Wiglaf replied, his tone jagged and tight. He swallowed. "There is a sheep, and the body of a boy. Both have been ripped and rent with great savagery. I've never seen anything like this. No wolf or bear would do this."

Octa squared his shoulders, choking back the bile that rose in his throat. He would not disgrace himself. His horse snorted, pulling away, so he handed his reins to Bassus. He moved closer to the corpse. He did not wish to look more closely, but Bassus had told him of the importance of knowing an enemy. To see how the shadow-walker had killed might prove useful come nightfall.

The sheep's innards were strewn over the path. Congealed blood and shit caked the hard, cold earth. Octa stepped over the guts and approached the corpse. He forced himself to kneel beside the bloody mess. The grass was wet and cold. White shards of splintered bone protruded from the chest. One leg was at an impossible angle. The shoe and leg wraps had been ripped off and now lay a few paces away, strewn on the grass. The stench of death filled his nose.

Octa closed his eyes. He did not want to look further. But he could sense the eyes of the other warriors on him. They were waiting. He cast his gaze once more over poor Breca's remains. The boy's kirtle and breeches were shredded tatters and stained brown. The twisted bare leg was missing several chunks of flesh that had seemingly been ripped away. The ribs appeared to have been ground and scraped clean of meat. No. Not scraped. Gnawed. He thought he could detect grooves made by teeth on the ribs.

He stood shakily. He had seen enough. But there was something else. He wished he had stayed on his horse.

For an instant, he thought he might win the battle with his stomach, but then, in a rush, he took two quick steps away from the corpse and vomited noisily. He spat and looked in disgust at the steaming puddle at his feet. He was full of shame and yet, when he looked up at Bassus and the others, there was no reproach on their faces.

"Do not be ashamed, Octa," said Bassus. "The sight and smell would be enough to unman many."

Octa wiped his mouth with the back of his hand.

"It is not that," he said, and spat again to be rid of the vile taste in his mouth.

"Then what?" asked Bassus.

"The boy's head is gone."

Four

It fell to the two youngest warriors to dig Breca's grave. Expecting to find the body, they had brought spades. The older men led the horses away from the stink of death, leaving Wiglaf and Octa to do the hard work. Banstan approached as they set about digging into the hard earth, but once again, Bassus stopped him.

"I want to see my Breca once more before you bury him," he said.

"No, Banstan," said Bassus in a soothing voice. "Remember him as he was in life. Take those sheep and return to Gefrin. If you leave now you will be there well before the setting of the sun. Tell our king that we mean to track the creature. When we find it, we will avenge Breca and all the others it has slain."

Banstan did not argue. Perhaps the mention of the setting sun was enough to goad him into action. He turned silently and made his way back up the hill, towards where his dog held the sheep in check.

Towards Gefrin, and safety.

Sweat plastered Octa's fair hair against his forehead. He pushed the iron-edged wooden blade of the shovel into the earth, levered up another clump of mud and lifted it to one side. Wiglaf worked from the other end of the grave. They both toiled in silence. Soon Octa's shoulders and back were aching. He dug quickly, wanting to be done with the task. But that would only mean he would need to touch Breca's corpse all the sooner. The thought filled him with revulsion.

When the hole was long and deep enough, Wiglaf and Octa stood for a moment, catching their breath. Octa stretched and rubbed the small of his back. Being tall, he had needed to stoop.

"Come, you two," said Bassus. "Get the boy in the ground so that we can find this bastard monster. Gram has found its tracks."

Octa looked to Wiglaf, who sighed and nodded.

Some of the greedier, or braver crows had returned to the corpse. Wiglaf threw a clod of earth at them, sending them cawing once more into the sky. Together, Octa and Wiglaf half-lifted and half-dragged Breca's remains into the grave, using his clothing as much as possible to avoid touching the cold skin. The sharp point of a splintered bone grazed the back of Octa's hand. He shuddered. Had the others seen? He looked at Wiglaf. He too was pale, grim-faced, jaw set. Octa glanced up hill. Banstan was gone, along with the sheep.

Gram came to the grave.

"I found this yonder," he said, placing both ends of a snapped spear into the grave beside Breca's mangled body. "He might be wanting it where he's going."

Octa and Wiglaf picked up their shovels once more and started filling in the shallow hole.

When the earth was packed down on the small mound, the five warriors stood huddled around the forlorn grave.

They stood in silence for a long while. Crows cried out at them from where they sat on the slope. They had returned to the sheep, covering it in black. Some of the birds flew lazily above their heads. Perhaps they were in search of more meat now that they had been robbed of their feast.

"Breca, we did not know you," said Bassus, "but we heard how you fought to defend your sheep and your father. You were a brave lad. You did what any man could do. You faced your enemy and died with a weapon in your hand. Woden will welcome you into his great hall. Perhaps one day we will meet you there."

Octa said nothing. His stomach was empty and his limbs quivered from the exertion. His mind was full of the sight of ripped flesh, splintered bones and blood-soaked clothes. The boy had been brave. The beast he had confronted must have been formidable. Octa hoped that Woden would accept Breca into his corpse hall. But would Woden want a shepherd boy?

And, if he did, how would a headless boy find his way there in the afterlife?

Five

"It will be dark soon," Bassus said. "We should seek shelter."

Octa was glad Bassus had spoken. The sun had dipped below the western hills and Octa did not wish to be out in the marsh after dark.

They had made good progress since leaving Breca to his rest, such as it was. Gram had spotted tracks leading into the woods and they had led their horses through the dense woodland while he followed the beast's trail. From time to time, there were spots of dark dry blood on trees or plants, whether from the creature or from meat he had carried away from Breca and the sheep, they could not tell.

Perhaps, thought Octa, the blood oozed from the head of the boy as it dangled, sightless, from the monster's grip.

After the thick cover of the trees, the land opened out. Moors led to Bebbanburg to the east and down towards the marshes, pools and dune-studded beaches further south. The night-walker's trail was clear there in the bright noonday sun. Flecks of dried slaughter-sweat on trampled grass marked the creature's passing. They could not lose it. They had mounted, cantering south and east. In the distance, the marshland was cloaked in a thin pall of mist.

They had been eager to find the creature and slay it.

Octa had looked about him as they rode towards the fens and ponds of the marsh. The sun had glistened from horse harness and the men's battle gear. The thrum of their steeds' hooves beat a solid, implacable rhythm. There, in the sun, surrounded by strong shield-brothers, it had seemed they could not fail in their quest. Five of Edwin's strongest and bravest gesithas against one creature who had until now preyed upon defenceless travellers and sheep. Octa could already imagine the songs the scops would sing of them when they returned with the beast's head.

Glory and battle-fame awaited them.

But that had been a long while hence. They had passed no living creature larger than a bird on their ride to the marsh and when the ground began to yield and squelch beneath the horses' hooves, they had halted.

The horses' breath steamed and billowed around them in the chill air. Gram had dismounted and examined the ground.

"The trail leads that way," he said, pointing eastward, into the mist-enshrouded marsh.

Far off in the distance, smoke drifted lazily from some dwelling, unseen in the mist. Octa wondered what kind of people would choose to live here when there was good land close by.

"We should make a camp here," Unferth had said. He had barely spoken on the journey and his voice croaked in his throat. He coughed and spat a gobbet of phlegm into the weeds that grew in a verdant tangle beside the path. His spittle hung from the leaves like glutinous cobwebs.

"Why should we wait?" Wiglaf had asked. "There is yet much light in the sky. Let us follow this foul creature into the mire, for surely its lair lies within."

Octa had said nothing. The misty land to the east unnerved him, but he would follow where Bassus led.

Bassus had looked about him at the warriors' expectant faces, then peered into the veil of mist that hung over the earth.

Octa's mount had stepped close to Unferth's horse, which seemed to have the same sour temperament as its rider. Unferth's stallion had nipped Octa's horse's rump, causing it to whinny and leap away. Octa had needed to wrestle with the reins and cling to his saddle to remain mounted.

"We should camp here and wait for tomorrow's dawn," Unferth had said, seemingly oblivious of his horse's actions.

Octa had glowered at the old thegn, but had bitten back his words of retort.

The commotion had seemed to help Bassus make up his mind.

"We will head into the swamp," he said, ignoring Unferth's snort of derision. "If we tarry here, who is to say the creature will not once again attack in the darkness? Edwin King would have no more of his people slain by this thing. We should find it before dusk. And slay the bastard."

It had seemed so simple then. But now, with the shadows long on the mist-swirled ground and the cold marsh water soaking their legs, Octa wished that they had listened to Unferth. They had quickly had to dismount and lead the horses. Their progress had been halting.

Unferth had said nothing when they had made their way into the marshland. His eyes glinted with disdain, but he had kept his thoughts to himself. Now, as they all shivered and huddled in the gathering dusk, he spoke up.

"Perhaps now is the time to make camp, eh?" he said. "Here in this puddle looks like a good spot. What say you, wise Bassus?"

Bassus glared at the older thegn.

"Let us try to reach the dwelling that lies to the south. Look, the smoke still rises above the mist. It does not look so far. We shall find shelter there."

Unferth let out a barking laugh which turned into a cough.

"Ever one to grasp at the thinnest of chances," he said. "Very well, lead on, wise one."

They trudged onwards towards the smoke that must have risen from a hearth fire. The promise of warmth and shelter, and perhaps fresh ale, drove them forward until the light became too faint for them to make out where they were going.

The marsh was redolent of decay; dark and hidden scents, as of death. The warriors' feet and the hooves of the horses churned the quagmire. Stagnant pools bubbled at their passing. All around them the swamp sighed and whispered like a living thing.

Octa sniffed the air. He could not detect woodsmoke.

"It is too dark to continue," he said. None of the others refuted his words. "We have already lost the creature's trail. Now we will have to make camp as best we can and wait till morning."

They found a tiny mound that was barely large enough for them and their horses. They tried to make themselves as comfortable as possible. They ate bread and chewed on strips of salted-beef they had brought with them. They huddled together and did not even attempt to light a fire. There was no wood to be found and everything they carried was soaked through.

As night drew its cloak about them, Wiglaf grumbled.

"Our byrnies will be eaten by the iron-rot after a day and night in this accursed place."

From the gloom, which was now so dark that Octa could scarcely discern the shape of his comrades, came the rasping voice of Unferth.

"I would not worry about your iron-knit shirt being eaten." His words lingered for a moment in the chill air. One of the horses snorted and stamped in the darkness. "I would worry more about camping at night in the domain of the shadow-stalker. We know he has a taste for man-flesh. We should worry more about not becoming his next meal."

Six

Octa awoke in the deepest part of the night. He had not thought it possible that he would be able to sleep. But as he had wrapped himself in his cloak, his muscles ached and his body trembled as much from exhaustion as from the cold.

Why had he woken? Was it his turn to keep watch? There was nobody shaking him awake. None of his companions were speaking.

All was still.

But something had woken him.

Without rising from where he lay, Octa opened his eyes. He was not surrounded by the total darkness he had expected. The moon was up. It was full and its cool glow washed middle earth in silver. The mist was thicker now, but the moonlight spread through it. Octa could see no further than a few paces from where he lay, but the world was wreathed in a glowing fog. The dark bulk of Bassus was nearby. His huge friend had his back to him. As he looked, Bassus moved his head, peering into the mists. It must be Bassus' watch.

So what had caused Octa to waken?

A piercing shriek ululated from the marsh. Octa started, but remained where he was. It was impossible to make out where the noise had come from. It seemed to echo in the fog.

Silence once more.

Then a howl, long and plaintive, rolled over the moonlit land. A scream followed. Was that the voice of a woman?

Octa shuddered and rose. The night was alive with mischief. He would not face it lying down.

Gram, Unferth and Wiglaf did not seem to have heard the noises. They remained huddled in their blankets and cloaks. The horses whickered and snorted, unsettled by the disturbances somewhere out there in the marsh. Octa picked his way carefully to the beasts and soothed them with a gentle touch. The night was again silent and still. The fog hung unmoving and thick all about them.

What lurked out there in the mists? Was the nihtgenga even now stalking the night, sniffing out its man-prey? Or had the screams been more of its victims? Perhaps its appetite would be sated?

Careful not to disturb the sleeping men, Octa walked to where Bassus sat. Just as he was about to touch his friend's shoulder to alert him of his presence, the giant thegn leapt to his feet, spun around and dragged his sword from its scabbard.

"Bassus, it is I, Octa." His whispered warning sounded loud and harsh in the stillness of the night. For an instant, Octa feared that Bassus would not heed his words and strike him down. After a long moment, where the only movement was their breath clouding before them, Bassus lowered his blade.

"By Woden's balls," panted Bassus, "I thought you were the shadow-goer. I almost spit you like a boar."

"I give thanks that you did not," replied Octa, moving closer to stand beside his friend and placing a hand on his shoulder. "I was awoken by the sounds. The screams and howls."

"They were close. Do you think that was the beast?"

"What else?" asked Octa. "Though I think I heard the cry of a woman too."

"Aye, I heard it." For a long while, they were both silent. Octa listened to the night, straining to hear further evidence of the night-stalker.

"Do you think we heard it killing again?" Octa said. "While we rested here, lost in the marsh?"

Bassus did not reply.

Octa quickly continued, "I did not mean to cast the blame on you, Bassus. I am sorry."

"There is nothing for it now. We cannot go back and change what we have done, we can only learn and move forward. All I hope now is that we find this beast tomorrow while the sun shines in the skies. We can never hope to fight it in the dark and mists of this gods-forsaken swamp."

"Can it truly be a son of this Cain that Paulinus spoke of? A giant monster, cursed by Paulinus' god?"

"Who can say?" replied Bassus, sheathing once more his sword. "Gram followed the thing's trail easily enough. He said it walked like a man, on two feet. And we know it eats meat, the way any creature does. I care not what it is, as long as we can slay it. There are many things that we cannot explain in this world, Octa. The priests say they can speak to the gods and can change the way of things with sacrifice and ceremonies, and that may be. I have never seen a god, or an elf, or a goblin. But if we can find this night-thing, I would wager my horse, my sword and all my wealth that it can be cut with sharp steel. I have never come across any foe that could not be made to bleed. And if it can bleed, we can kill it."

They fell silent. The horses again began to stamp and snort. The squelching sound of a footfall in the mire. A whimpering moan from the moonlit misty gloom.

As one, Octa and Bassus drew their blades.

Another groan. A splash. Snuffling. Something large was out there in the night. Something stealthy. Deadly.

"Show yourself," Octa said. His voice was loud and clear. To his surprise, he sounded confident to his own ears. Behind him, he heard the others rising rapidly, woken by his words.

"Is it out there?" Wiglaf called in a breathless voice.

"Quiet," said Bassus.

Wiglaf, Gram and Unferth joined them at the edge of the small knoll. They all stared into the moon-tinged fog, searching, listening.

Was that a shadow in the mist that Octa saw? One of the horses whinnied. There was another splash, very near this time. A guttural grunting.

Sweat prickled Octa's brow despite the cold night air. At any moment, the creature would burst from the mist and rip them apart, byrnies and weapons and all. Nothing could protect them from the beast that stalked them in the night.

"Show yourself," Bassus said, repeating Octa's words. "Come on, you bastard. Come and fight some real men. There are no shepherds and boys here. We are warriors of King Edwin and we are your doom. Step out from where you cower and face us."

The warriors tightened their grips on their weapons and girded themselves for the attack that was sure to follow their leader's goading words.

But no attack came. No creature, all fangs and claws, came leaping for them from the gloom. Instead a rumbling sound came to them. At first, Octa was unsure what he was hearing, and then he remembered Banstan's words in the hall. What he heard now was the boulder-rub chuckle of the nihtgenga.

The monster was laughing.

Seven

They slept no more that night. They stood for a long while, each straining to see something in the mist, but nothing came. The laughter had ceased and no further sounds came from the marsh, save for the hoot of an owl way off to the north. After a time, the men sat, back to back, on the crest of the small mound.

"Do you think it has gone?" asked Wiglaf.

"Quiet, boy," rasped Unferth. "If you prattle, we will not hear it should it return."

And so they had sat in chilled silence, each lost in his own thoughts and fears. It would soon be Geola, midwinter, so the night was long. The darkness dragged on until Octa wondered if it would ever be light. Geola was not a time to be huddled in a swamp. It was a time for warm fires. Hot food and good company. Was it this cold in Cantware, he mused? He could picture his sisters preparing the Geola honey cakes with their mother. Beobrand carrying logs in from outside and placing them on the roaring blaze on the hearthstone. Their father, Grimgundi would be sitting on his fine polished seat, as he often did, dark, brooding and drunk, emanating violence the way the fire gave off heat. In his mind's eye, Octa could clearly see their faces, red and shadowy from the flames. He missed them.

All except for Grimgundi. He hoped he would never see his father again.

He shivered, pushing thoughts of his father from his mind. Octa felt the usual stab of guilt at having left his brother and sisters behind with the brute, but he could not dwell upon the past. All he could think of was finding some respite from the chill. Seldom had he been so cold. The water seeped from the very earth they sat upon, further soaking already wet breeches. His teeth chattered and he wrapped his arms around his chest, with each hand wedged under an arm for warmth. He had placed his seax on the wet ground before him. Iron-rot be damned. He wanted the blade close to hand should the creature come back.

At last a pale red light began to tinge the fog, mottling the dawn air like the skin of a salmon, all pinks and greys. Octa could imagine the sun rising over the sea to the east, but here, in the swamp, its rays hardly penetrated. Slowly, the warriors rose stiffly, stretching muscles that had grown taut with cold and inactivity. The mists swirled and eddied like smoke as they moved about the knoll, preparing the horses to leave.

"I hope this fog lifts," said Wiglaf, voicing the worry of all of them.

"The sun will surely burn it away by midmorning," said Bassus, his voice self-assured and firm. Octa wished he shared his confidence.

34

No warmth came from the sun. They hobbled and coughed like old greybeards as they readied themselves. Soon the horses were ready, and they looked to Bassus once more to lead them. Unferth's expression was sour. Bassus was not young, but Unferth was older than the rest. The cold long night must have made his bones ache. Octa expected some reproach from the old warrior, but Unferth kept his mouth firmly shut.

Bassus looked about them. Enough light filtered through the mists for them to travel, but they could not see beyond a dozen paces in any direction.

"Let us try to find those dwellings," said Bassus. "We saw their smoke and we cannot be that far from them. They were southward and the sun helps us to mark our path in that direction."

Nobody replied, but they set off into the pools and channels of the marsh, with the sun's ruddy glow to their left. It was hard going. The water was gelid, with films of ice on many of the puddles and ponds. Octa wondered absently why some were frozen but not others. But he was too chilled to care.

They had travelled only a very short way when Gram, who led them, let out a cry of alarm.

"By Woden, Tiw and Thunor!"

In a splashing chaos they all rushed forward to aid him. Without thinking, Octa dragged his seax from its scabbard and, letting go of his horse's reins, he half waded and half ran to Gram's side.

Eight

"What is it?" cried Wiglaf. "Is the beast here?"

Gram did not answer immediately. They gathered about him, their panting breath steaming.

Octa shouldered his way past Unferth and Wiglaf. A moment later, he wished he had not done so.

There was no creature here to attack them, but it was now clear what they had heard in the night.

For looming out of the fog was the face of a young man. Breca, Octa assumed. The severed head of the boy had been set atop a wooden shaft which had been driven into the soft earth of a knoll, very like the one where they had camped.

The face was hideous, the eyes bulged, the tongue lolled from the blue-lipped mouth. Shreds of gore dangled from the neck, as if the head had been torn from Breca's shoulders.

Octa was the first to break the silence.

"Is the night-walker toying with us?" Was there a hint of despair in his tone?

"Perhaps," answered Gram. "Or mayhap this is a warning. Come no further into my domain…"

"Who can say?" Bassus' gravelly voice was strong and as obdurate as granite. "I think it is mocking us. Now there is only one thing we can be certain of."

"What," asked Wiglaf.

"This night-crawling bastard beast is as good as dead. Nobody and nothing makes a jest of me and lives to tell the tale."

Nine

They continued south.

"We should take it... the head... Take it back and bury it with the rest of the boy," Wiglaf had said before they had left.

Unferth had snorted.

"You can carry that head if you wish. I'll not be touching it. The boy's dead. Leave him be now."

"But... he is not whole..." Wiglaf's voice had trailed off. None of the others had made a move towards the pitiful-looking head. At last, Wiglaf had turned to follow them, leaving the grisly totem behind.

Octa shuddered, only partly from the cold. The sightless eyes of the boy had unnerved him. They should have done as Wiglaf said. Perhaps Breca's spirit would never find its way to the afterlife now. Would he forever wander this mist-shrouded marsh in search of his body? But it was too late now. They had splashed and waded quite some way and the fog had not lifted. They could not have returned to the stake and the head even if they had wanted to. They were lost. None of them had said the words, but Octa was sure they all thought it. He was on the verge of speaking up, proposing that they head west towards the hills and dry land, and out of this dismal swamp, when a sobbing cry came to them on the still air.

They loosened weapons in their scabbards and reached for amulets. Unferth spat.

Wiglaf's horse skidded, its hooves slipping in the greasy mire. The animal slid into the young warrior, knocking him forward. Wiglaf cursed and shook the beast's reins.

"Quiet," hissed Bassus.

They stood still and listened.

"There," whispered Octa, "Did you hear it?"

None of them said a word, but their drawn faces spoke for them. They all heard the crying whimper from the mist-murk.

Bassus slowly pulled his sword from its scabbard. Octa, trusting their leader's instinct, drew his own blade. The seax felt very small in his hand. He wished he owned a sword like that of the older thegns. One day, he hoped, but for now, the sharp, single-edged dagger would need to do.

Slowly, making as little noise as possible, they moved towards the sounds of distress.

"Wait," whispered Gram, reaching out his hand to halt Bassus.

The huge thegn frowned.

"What?"

"Listen."

Again they stood and strained to make sense of what they heard.

"I can hear nothing," said Unferth, spitting again.

"Your ears are old, Unferth," said Bassus. "Let the young lads tell us what they hear."

Unferth glowered at Bassus, but said nothing.

"It is a woman's weeping," said Wiglaf at last.

"You are certain?" asked Bassus.

Wiglaf cocked his head and held his breath for a moment. He nodded.

"Aye."

Octa could hear it too now. The plaintive sobs of a woman's sorrow.

"Come," said Bassus, "let us see who this woman is and what she weeps for."

They sloshed and squelched on once more, the cold fingers of the mud pulling at their feet and legs, as if the very swamp did not wish to see them leave.

Octa noticed that Bassus did not sheathe his blade.

After a time, the ground began to rise. The sounds of crying were clear now. There were other voices too. Now and again they could make out words. As they stumbled out of the chill waters of the marsh, a voice came clear and loud to them. A man's voice, calling out.

"Wealhtheow!" the voice bellowed. "Wealhtheow!"

For a moment, the warriors stood shivering. There was no reply to the man's calls. The weeping grew more intense.

"Hail!" Bassus spoke into the mists. "Hail there."

Silence for a heartbeat.

"Who is it that comes from the marsh? Show yourself."

"I am Bassus, son of Nechten, thegn of Edwin, who is king of these lands. My companions and I mean you no harm, but we are wet and cold and would ask for your hospitality. Somewhere to dry ourselves, perhaps something to eat."

No reply.

"We will pay," said Bassus.

The sobbing had ceased.

"Come here where I can see you then," said the man.

They climbed the slight slope. The mist thinned and Octa felt sunlight on his cheek.

Before them huddled a small group of huts. Roofed with sods, walls daubed in earth. They seemed to be growing from the ground itself. Woodsmoke drifted from the largest building, mingling with the mist.

The man who had spoken stood brandishing a large axe. He was massive, easily a head taller than Bassus and Octa, who were the tallest warriors of Edwin's retinue. The man's face was hidden by a thick thatch of dark beard, and his hair was shaggy and long. Around his shoulders he wore a thick bear pelt. For a moment, it seemed to Octa that they were approaching a huge, axe-wielding bear. He was glad he yet held his seax in his hand. But what good would such a small blade do against this brute with the giant axe?

The man's eyes widened when he took in their numbers, their horses and their fine weapons. Behind the man cowered a woman, she whimpered and whined as she peeked past his bulk.

Bassus sheathed his sword, signalling for the others to do the same. Octa felt a pang of worry as he slid his seax back into its wood-and-leather scabbard.

"I have told you my name," said Bassus, "now tell me yours."

"I am Hrothgar," he spoke as one who needed no introduction, like a lord in his hall. "This is my wife, Modthrith." He nodded towards the woman.

The woman was plain of face. Tears had streaked the grime on her cheeks. Her red-rimmed eyes flicked from one thegn to the next, missing nothing. There was a hard cunning in those eyes that made Octa wonder what could cause one such as this to sob and weep like a maid.

"You spoke of payment," said Hrothgar, his eyes glinting in the sunlight that was pushing its way through the mist.

"We have coin," said Bassus.

"Coin?" Hrothgar hawked and spat. "What use do I have for a sliver of metal here?"

Octa glanced around them at the collection of hovels that squatted on this small mound in the marsh. Hrothgar had a point.

"I will give you coin, Hrothgar, in exchange for shelter and food," replied Bassus in a tone that would broach no argument. His hand fell to his sword's pommel and he leaned forward. "We are cold and hungry and a clever man would invite his king's men into his home before haggling over payment for the hospitality that is theirs by right."

For a moment, Octa thought that Hrothgar would refuse them. His gnarled hands clenched on his axe haft, the knuckles whitening under the dark hair that bristled there.

"And," Bassus continued, his voice softer now, "a wise man would know that he could trade coin for other things of more use to him. A knife perhaps. Good cloth. A jewel for his goodwife."

Hrothgar's brows pulled down into a scowl. Eventually he nodded, but he did not move.

"What are you doing in the marsh?" he asked. "Why have you come to this place? Have you come from the sea?"

"No. We are come from the great hall of Gefrin. A creature came there in the night and slew a shepherd boy. We have tracked it back to this swamp."

Hrothgar looked sharply at Modthrith, who let out a whimper. Octa thought she might swoon.

"You know of this creature?" Octa asked. "This nihtgenga?"

Modthrith's tears began to flow once more. Hrothgar absently patted her head in comfort. He lowered his axe, resting its great iron head on the ground at his feet, as if deciding that these thegns were not his enemies.

"Aye," Hrothgar said, "we know of it." His voice was as a wasteland where nothing lived. "It has stalked the marsh for many nights now. Of course we know of it."

Modthrith's crying grew stronger, her sobbing louder.

"Aye, we know it," the great bear of a man continued. "It came here last night and stole away our daughter."

Ten

Octa grunted with pleasure as he emptied his full bladder. The hot stream of piss splashed and splattered into the brackish waters of the marsh. They had drunk Hrothgar's ale for much of the afternoon. It was sour and weak, and had a faint taste of fish about it, but after the first cup the flavour seemed to matter little. They had questioned Hrothgar, Modthrith and their two sons, Heorogar and Hondscio, but had learnt little of use. They were all tight-lipped, barely talking unless pressed. It seemed they eked out their living here catching eels and birds. A hard life, but few could choose how they lived. It was Hrothgar's wyrd and that of his family to dwell in a swamp fishing for eels with wicker baskets and trapping the ducks and sandpipers with cunningly rigged nets.

But despite their mean existence and sour ale, Hrothgar had been as good as his word. Modthrith had fed them a thin stew of fish and their small hut was warm enough. After the long cold night in the marsh, it felt wonderful to feel the warmth of a fire thaw the limbs.

Octa finished pissing and pulled up his breeches. The mists had thinned in the afternoon, but the warriors had not felt ready to head out once more into the marsh. Besides, they had no idea where the creature could be found. Bassus had asked Hrothgar where the nihtgenga came from, but the man had shrugged, and said nothing.

"We will seek out this beast at first light," Bassus had said. Hrothgar had taken a swig of his fishy ale, remaining silent. "If your daughter, Wealhtheow, yet lives, we will bring her back to you."

Modthrith had drawn in a ragged breath.

Octa had seen Bassus' eyes then in the smoky hut. Neither of them believed they would find the girl alive. From Modthrith's sobbing, it seemed neither did she.

Octa looked now to the west. The last rays of the dying sun yet tinted the sky with red. It would be dark soon. In Gefrin they would be pulling shutters closed, preparing for the evening meal. He wondered what Elda was doing. He missed her quick smile and swaying hips. He was sure she watched him too, but he had seen her talking to Hengist. What of it? They were not betrothed. He resolved to approach her when he returned. He pulled his cloak about his shoulders. He wished Elda was here to keep him warm. The wool of his cloak was still damp, not yet fully-dried by the warmth of Hrothgar's hut. He turned, meaning to return to where he could hear the voices of the men.

A hulking shape barred his way.

Jumping back, Octa scrabbled for his seax. How could he have been so stupid? The ale had fogged his mind.

"Easy now, Octa," said the deep voice of Bassus. "I would rather you did not gut me like one of Hrothgar's eels."

Octa let out a long breath that steamed in the cool evening.

Chuckling, Bassus stepped past Octa and began to relieve himself.

Octa's heart hammered. He took a slow, calming breath. The stink of piss mingled with the marsh's rank redolence of decay. Octa's stomach churned.

"We should set watches tonight," he said, glad that his voice did not waver.

"Aye," said Bassus. "And we need to stop drinking Hrothgar's fish-piss ale. The beast could come upon us now and take our heads and we would not notice."

They trudged slowly back to the hut.

"Do you trust him?" Octa asked in a whisper.

"Hrothgar? No. He'd kill us just as surely as any night creature. I saw the way he coveted our horses and weapons. Which is why we will watch in pairs tonight. First Gram and you, then Unferth and Wiglaf, then me and Hrothgar."

"You think he'll agree to take a watch?"

"I'd like to see him refuse me," answered Bassus.

They were almost at the door now. From inside came the sound of Wiglaf's voice, high and clear as he told a tale to Hrothgar's young sons.

"What of Heorogar and Hondscio?"

"They are mere pups. Best they stay inside with their mother."

Octa paused before opening the door.

"Do you think the creature will return tonight?" he asked.

Bassus rubbed a hand over his beard. His eyes were grim in the gathering darkness.

"I do not know, lad," he said. "But I hope so."

"You do?"

"Aye. We know we will have to kill it in the end. Just as well we could do it without having to spend another day traipsing through this accursed swamp."

Bassus swung the door open, letting out a waft of hot, fishy air into the cold evening.

Octa shuddered. Placing his hand on the antler handle of his seax he peered out into the mists for a long while, before turning away from the chill gloom and stepping through the threshold of Hrothgar's home.

Eleven

Screams.

And a clashing chaos of sounds.

Octa leapt up from where he had lain beside the warm embers of the hearth. He had hardly slept. It felt as though he had barely closed his eyes after his long, chill watch. His mind was dull, leaden from tiredness and the rancid ale he had consumed the night before. His hand already gripped his seax. He had not sheathed it to sleep.

Around him all was frenzy. Too many men for the small hut were struggling from their slumber all at once. Curses and cries from within the darkness of the hovel were added to the cacophony outside.

Another scream ripped the night air.

Octa leapt for the door and flung it open. The cold fog of the night roiled into the hut. Standing in the doorway was a shadowy figure. For a moment, Octa was poised to strike. But the cold air brought him to his senses like a slap. This was no night creature.

"Unferth," Octa said, "what's happened?"

"To arms!" yelled Unferth, at last finding his voice. "To arms! The creature is abroad and Wiglaf is fallen."

Bassus, Hrothgar and Gram shoved their way past Octa and into the night.

"Where?" snapped Bassus.

Unferth did not reply, but he pointed to the west. The moon was high and the mist-draped land was alight with a silvery glow.

The men rushed off.

"Come, show us," said Octa, urging Unferth forward with a push.

But Unferth would not return into the fog. His face was white in the darkness. White streaked with black. Blood. Octa pushed him once more. Unferth was garbed in a battle-knit shirt, and bore a fine sword.

"Come, we need your strength, Unferth."

But the old thegn shook his head.

Seeing it was pointless to insist, Octa grabbed Unferth's right wrist and with his other hand wrenched the sword from his grasp. Best that the blade be put to use, rather than left in the hut where Modthrith and her children cowered.

Shoving Unferth away, Octa sprinted after the others. The heft of the sword felt strange but welcome in his hand.

A terrible roar of anger and sounds of struggle in the fog. Octa ran on.

And then he saw them. Bassus, Gram and Hrothgar brandished their weapons. Moonlight flickered on the blades. Before them crouched a huge beast. Shaggy fur covered its massive bulk. It was hunkered over a body.

A corpse. Wiglaf.

The young warrior's shocked face dangled from the nihtgenga's paw. Like Breca, the head had been ripped from the corpse's body. Wiglaf had been Octa's friend. He was quick and clever, with thoughts as fast as flashes of lightning from a brooding, still sky. But now he was slain; taken by this beast. Wiglaf's eyes stared out from the gore-slathered face.

Without pause to think, Octa raised Unferth's sword and launched himself at the foul creature. He bellowed, releasing his own beast from within. The animal rage that he kept locked deep within himself. That fury had now broken its chains and nothing would calm it, save for blood.

The night-stalker, with a speed that belied its size, flung the head to one side and brought itself up to its full height. It towered over Octa now, who flew at the beast and was unable to alter his attack. The sword-blow that he had hoped would take the monster's head now hammered into its chest.

It was like hitting rock. A flash of sparks briefly lit the gloom. The thrum of the blade rang up Octa's arm. His wrist went numb from the impact. Such a strike should have buried itself deep within the beast's flesh. Maybe even cleaved it in two. But the nihtgenga scarcely stumbled. It let out a grunt and then clubbed Octa with a fist like iron. Octa fell back into the mud, his lip split. He tasted blood. His head was once more clouded. Lights flashed before his eyes. He struggled to rise. Everything was blurred. Sounds were louder than they should be.

Bassus let out a roar and rushed towards the creature, Gram a heartbeat behind him. Octa shook his head to clear it. He must help his friends. He pushed himself to his knees, spitting blood into the mud. His hand found the hilt of the sword that he had dropped. Shakily, he stood.

Bassus and Gram yet battled with the beast. Hrothgar, almost as tall as the shadow-walker, was still, hanging back from the fray. Without warning, Gram hurtled back into Hrothgar and they both fell in a tangle of limbs. Bassus faced the monster alone. Octa shook his head once more. He was still dizzy, but he could not leave his friend to fight this thing unaided.

Gripping the sword tightly, he stepped forward.

"Hey!" Octa shouted. "I haven't finished with you yet, you ugly whoreson."

For an instant, the creature's head swung towards the sound. Bassus seized his chance and thrust his blade low. He must have hit his mark, for the beast let out a wailing howl, almost like that of a child. Bassus made to press home his attack. But the creature, even injured, was as fast as thought. It leapt away and was swallowed by the fog. They heard splashing, retreating into the distance. And then, the night was still once more.

Octa reached out a hand and helped Gram to his feet. They ignored Hrothgar, who seemed dazed, sitting in the muck.

They approached Bassus, who was staring at the body at his feet.

For a time they stood, panting from the fight.

"Poor Wiglaf," said Octa. "We will bury him whole." He bent to the corpse and removed the cloak. Then, gently, with trembling hands he placed Wiglaf's head on the wool. He wrapped the head with care. He was glad when he could no longer see those shocked eyes.

"Aye," said Bassus, "poor Wiglaf that he should stand as warden with one who is craven." Neither Octa nor Gram replied. Ire washed off Bassus like the stench of rotting plants from the swamp.

"You injured it," said Gram.

Bassus looked down at the sword in his hand. The blade was slick with dark blood.

His teeth flashed white in the darkness.

"It bleeds like a man," he said.

"That was no man," said Octa, recalling the jolting pain in his wrist as his sword struck.

"Whatever it is," said Bassus, "it bleeds and it will die. I swear my oath to Woden, All-Father. We will follow this shadow-stalker to its lair when the sun rises and I will slay it."

Behind them, Hrothgar finally snapped out of his daze and moaned.

Twelve

They were ready to leave as the sun rose. A cold wind blew from the east, shredding the mist. From the slight elevation of Hrothgar's steading, they could see far into the marsh. In the distance, the land rose again before reaching the coast. Without the vale of fog, they would be able to pick their way through the fens and pools.

From the edge of the marsh Gram smiled grimly and nodded to Bassus. The beast's tracks were clear and dark spatters of blood from his wound showed where it had passed.

"You can follow it?" Bassus asked.

"Aye. With clear skies, we should be able to run it to ground today."

Bassus turned to Hrothgar, who seemed somehow smaller in the grey dawn light. His shoulders were hunched, his eyes downcast.

"We will leave the horses here," Bassus said. "They are in your care. If anything should happen to them, it will be you who will pay. They are from the king's stables and he is not a forgiving man. See that nothing befalls them."

Hrothgar nodded, but did not speak. Ever since the fight in the darkness, he had changed. Gone was the belligerent, gruff man who demanded payment for his hospitality. Instead he was meek and nervous, like a hound that has been kicked too many times. His wife and sons seemed to have also been shocked into silence. Modthrith had served them some chewy bread and salted eels with more fishy ale without uttering a sound. But all the while her eyes moved, taking in everything. She unnerved Octa.

"Ready?" said Bassus, in a loud voice.

Octa nodded.

Bassus clapped him on the shoulder.

"Good," said Bassus. "Let us find this bastard creature and slay it. It has brought too much death and misery. Gram, lead on."

He did not pause to look at Unferth.

When they had returned to the hovel in the night, Bassus had taken one of their shovels and thrust it savagely into Unferth's chest. The old thegn had seemed bemused at first, but after a moment he had grasped the wooden haft.

"Bury Wiglaf whole," Bassus had said. "And bury him deep."

Unferth had not spoken. With lowered head he had left the hut.

Octa waited for him now. Unferth walked stiffly from the grave he had dug. His face was drawn, the sickly grey of a trout's belly.

"Come, Unferth," said Octa. "Do not blame yourself. Wiglaf's death was not your doing."

He placed a hand on Unferth's arm, but the older man shrugged it off and brushed past him without a word.

They made good progress through the marsh. Gram was able to follow the beast's trail easily. The breeze in their faces brought tears to their eyes and Octa's swollen, scabbed lip throbbed in the cold. But the lack of fog made the going so much easier than the previous days. They did not slip and slide blindly into frigid pools and foul-smelling quagmires, instead they carefully chose their steps, moving from one tussock of marsh grass to the next. In this way, they managed to keep quite dry. Octa could scarcely believe they had been lost for so long in such a small expanse of land. The sun was still far from its zenith when the earth underfoot became drier, more solid.

As the ground rose, they paused. Looking back, Octa could see the thin trail of smoke from Hrothgar's hearth.

"Did we really wander lost in that marsh?" he said, more to himself than the others.

Bassus frowned.

"It must be cursed," he said. "We could walk from one end to the other in the time it takes to give a woman a good ploughing."

"I fear we would not get far in the time it takes you to swive a wench," said Gram.

Bassus snorted, but did not respond to the taunt. The attempt to lift their spirits had failed. None of them laughed.

Turning to Gram, he asked: "Where is the creature headed?"

Gram studied the grass on the ground that rose towards the east. The scent of the sea was on the air. Gulls careened in the sky.

"The nihtgenga did not alter course," Gram said. "It went straight up this bluff."

They pressed on.

"If the gods smile on us," said Gram, "we might run the monster to ground while this sun yet shines. Or," he bent to the ground, placing his hand on something and then raising it for them all to behold, "perhaps Bassus' blow has finished the creature and we will find it dead." The hand he showed them was red with the slaughter-dew of the beast's passing.

They nodded and carried on. But Octa did not believe it was their wyrd to find the creature dead. They would face the shadow-stalker again, he was sure of it. It felt as though they were living out a tale of someone else's telling and there was nothing they could do to change it. The swamp trapping them and leading them to Hrothgar's steading. The creature attacking in the night. Wiglaf's death. Even Bassus wounding it and the trail of blood out of the marsh. He could feel the threads of their wyrd being inexorably entwined and twisted with that of this fell beast.

He spat and reached for the Thunor hammer he wore. He winced as the scab on his lip split open once more. Was the creature even now watching them? There were clumps of thrift and some stunted sea buckthorns clinging to this wind-swept slope, but there was nowhere for such a huge thing to hide.

The sound of the wind grew louder. The distant crash of surf. The screech of gulls.

The warriors had reached the end of the creature's trail. They stood at the edge of the land. Far below them, waves rolled into rocks, sending up sheets of spray. Out to sea were dotted the Farena islands. The earth dropped away in a sheer cliff down to the jagged rocks and sand of a small beach.

"Well," said Bassus, asking the very question in Octa's thoughts, "where did the bastard go?"

Gram, cautious not to slip, leaned over the edge of the precipice. After a long while he rose and returned to where they had gathered some way from the edge. His mouth twisted in a strange expression.

"What?" asked Bassus.

"I think," Gram answered, with a frown, "the bastard went over the edge."

Thirteen

The wind lashed at Octa. His fingers were already numb from the cold, but he could not stop to warm them. His cloak billowed, tugging at him, threatening to pull him from the cliff-face to his doom. He glanced down. So far yet to go. This was madness. They should have stayed at the top. They would be no use to King Edwin or anyone else if they tumbled to their deaths, smashed and bloody on the rocks at the base of the cliff.

Gritting his teeth, Octa felt for another foothold with his toes. He kicked out detritus from a small niche, the remains of an old nest, and lowered himself down a little further.

"There is a cave down there," Gram had said shortly before, and they had all gathered precariously at the edge of the cliff. Staring down, they had seen that Gram spoke true. There was a shadowed opening far below them. This must be the beast's lair.

"We cannot climb down there," Unferth had said, speaking for the first time since Wiglaf's death. His face was pallid and drawn, the same colour as his greying beard.

"What else should we do," Bassus had retorted. "We must kill the beast, or see that it is dead before we return to the king. There is yet much sun in the sky. Would you rather wait till nightfall?"

Unferth had quailed at that, perhaps recalling the huge bulk of the beast looming in the darkness.

"We have no rope," Octa had offered.

"There are many rocks and ledges to help us climb down," Bassus had said confidently, but now, with the chill wind buffeting him and his fingers and toes senseless from the cold, Octa wondered whether they had once again fallen foul of their leader's overconfidence.

They had left Unferth atop the cliff.

"I will keep watch here. I am not strong enough for the descent," he had said, his voice small. "I am not the man I once was."

Octa felt for the man, but Bassus had spat over the cliff.

"Give your sword to Octa, that it may be put to good use by a warrior," he had said, disdain dripping from his words. Octa had returned the sword to the old thegn the night before, but now Unferth removed his belt and handed the scabbarded blade to him.

"This sword is called Hrunting," Unferth had said. "It was a gift from King Edwin when I was a younger man. A finer blade has never been forged. Treat it well, young Octa, and bring it back to me."

Octa had accepted the sword.

"It is a fine, true blade, Unferth. I pray that I will kill the beast with it, that it will add to its glory. I will return it to you, if I yet draw breath."

A pebble rattled down the cliff and hit Octa's head with a painful thwack.

"By Thunor's cock," came the shout of surprise and fear from above.

Looking up, Octa saw that Bassus had lost his footing. For a heartbeat, the massive thegn dangled from his fingertips, feet flailing for purchase. More stones showered down and Octa turned his face away. He gritted his teeth and pushed himself into the wall. If Bassus should fall, he would surely take Octa with him. But no hurtling body came to dislodge him from his perch. Octa opened his eyes and looked up once more. Bassus had found a ledge for his feet. He grinned at Octa.

"This is better than being cooped up with the womenfolk for Geola, eh?" Bassus laughed.

Octa shook his head. Would it be his wyrd to die thus? To fall from a cliff in this northern land? Hardly the thing of songs.

Clenching his jaw, he continued down.

Grey and white-feathered gulls wheeled past, swooping in close, screeching at these intruders to their rocky domain. To Octa it sounded as if they were laughing.

Reaching out to place his hand into a small crack, Octa noticed something. A dark brown stain unlike the white droppings of the birds. Dried blood. The nihtgenga had descended this way. He looked down, suddenly fearful that the beast was there below them, ready to pounce, or perhaps climbing up towards them in animal leaps and bounds.

But there was nothing below save the rocks, the sand, the waves. And the cave mouth, yawning into the belly of the cliff.

The cliff was in shadow, and the sea wind made it bitterly cold. Several more times Octa feared that he, or one of the others would fall. But at last his feet crunched into the sand and pebbles and he stared up, as Bassus and Gram made their way down the last stretch of crumbling rock.

Behind him, waves crashed onto jagged teeth of rocks that jutted from the surf. The spray was as cold as chips of ice. He pulled his cloak about him and rubbed his hands, trying to bring feeling back to them. At the top of the cliff, Octa could make out the grey face of Unferth peering down to see how they fared. Octa raised his hand, and Unferth responded in the same way.

Bassus and Gram both completed the descent and stood beside Octa, gazing up the shadowed cliff. Clouds had gathered in the sky now. The thought of making that climb in the rain caused a shudder down Octa's spine.

"Well, we made it," said Bassus. He stretched and worked his arms, removing the tension that had built up there. Putting his gnarled hands behind his head, he pulled, making his neck crack. Thus prepared, the tall thegn drew his blade and turned towards the great gash in the rock-face. The cave where the beast must surely dwell.

Gram, seemingly undaunted by the cold, the long climb down or the prospect of facing the monster in the dark, drew his own sword.

Octa pulled Hrunting from its scabbard and for a moment marvelled at the serpent-like patterns on the blade. His hands shook. He hoped the others did not notice.

"May the gods smile upon us now," Bassus said, and led the way into the rocky maw.

Fourteen

The cave was dark, the rocks sea-slick underfoot. The crash and thump of the breaking waves was loud behind them as they slowly shuffled into the opening in the cliff. Icy sea spray splattered around and on the warriors. The cold wind gusted, pushing them forward with invisible hands. Kelp squelched as they passed. Octa slipped and fell hard. Hrunting clattered from his grip and his hands scraped against limpets and barnacles.

Cursing inwardly, he leapt to his feet, snatching up the fine sword from where it had fallen.

The three men hesitated, awaiting the beast that would surely leap from the gloom to fight them. But nothing came.

Octa let out his pent-up breath. Once more they stepped forward into the darkness.

A pool, teeming with anemones and bladderwrack filled the entrance. After a moment vainly searching for a dry path, Bassus stepped into the water. He eased his foot down, unsure of the depth or what might lurk within the weeds. But the water only came up to just above his ankle. He placed his other foot into the pool and stepped on.

Octa and Gram followed him closely. The water was chill. Octa shuddered.

Without speaking they carried on into the shadows under the earth. After the pool, the ground rose and the opening turned to the left. There was only space for one of them to pass at a time. This is where the beast would attack. An ambush now and Bassus would be struck down before Gram or Octa could close with the monster. Bassus turned to look at them for a moment. His face was grim, but his eyes shone in the reflected light of the grey afternoon sky. He nodded and stepped past the rocky doorway and into the cavern.

There was no scream. No sudden smash and clamour of battle.

Octa hurried forward, with Gram close behind.

As they moved beyond the entrance and into the cave-gloom, the sounds of the sea and wind faded, swallowed by the earth. In the sudden stillness, Octa looked about him, his eyes flicking quickly around the cavern for signs of danger. His eyes grew accustomed to the darkness quickly. Enough light filtered through the cave mouth to clearly illumine the secrets of the dank domain of the nihtgenga.

There was no sign of the huge creature they had faced in battle the night before, but there was no doubt now that this was the lair of the foul creature. Over the scent of brine and seaweed, lay the heavy, sickly stench of rotting flesh. There was a splash of white in the gloom. Was it bird shit on the rocks? Unusual for birds to venture into a cave. Octa took a tentative step closer. All of a sudden, his mind made sense of what he was seeing and he drew in a sudden breath.

Not bird droppings. No. The skull of a man.

Dark hair still clung to it, but there was no skin, leaving the pale bone to shine through. Three other heads, each in differing stages of decomposition rested alongside the bare-bone skull. The black eye sockets in the grimacing faces seemed to be watching them. The heads were nestled on a ledge of stone some way up the cave wall. Beneath them lay a jumble of branches. No, not branches. Bones. He did not wish to approach those grisly remains of the monster's victims, but Octa was sure that should he pick up one of those bones and examine it in a bright light, he would find the same patterns of gnawing they had seen on Breca's ribs.

His stomach twisted and for a heartbeat he was sure that he would puke.

"The creature is not here," Gram said, his voice echoing in the rocky chamber.

Octa pulled his gaze from the gruesome onlookers on the stone shelf and looked around the cave. Gram was right. The cavern was not much larger than a poor family's hut. The dim light from the entrance was enough to see that the night-stalker was nowhere to be seen. Some way into the cave, on a small expanse of sand, lay the remains of a small fire. Octa knelt beside the charred wood and ash. He blew softly onto the embers and they glowed red in the darkness.

"Still hot," he said.

A small sound made him look up sharply. He raised Unferth's sword and stood quickly.

"What was that?" he asked, peering into the deepest recesses of the cavern. "Who's there?" He heard Bassus and

Gram both stepping forward to lend their support on either side of him. Octa did not look away from where the sound had emanated.

There was someone, or something, in this cave with them. His knuckles whitened as he grasped Hrunting's grip. From outside came the whispers of crashing surf and sea birds crying on the wind.

"Who's there?" he asked again, and took a step forward. Bassus and Gram followed him further into the cavern.

A movement then. A rustle of cloth. The three warriors crouched, ready to fend off attack. But still none came.

And then they saw her, huddled and hidden beneath a great bear pelt. Perhaps she had been sleeping and had awoken at the sound of their voices. She stared out at them now from the warmth of her fur-nest. Her eyes were large, limpid and lambent; her cheeks smooth and pale as polished stone.

"Wealhtheow?" Octa said. For surely this must be the girl that the beast had taken. But how did she yet live?

A flicker of recognition in those huge eyes perhaps? But she did not reply.

"Speak girl," said Bassus, not unkindly, "are you hale?"

Again, no response.

"Where is the creature?" Octa tried, but he was once more met with silence.

"How are we to get her up that cliff?" Gram asked. "Can you climb?"

Octa thought he made out a small movement of her head, but still she did not speak. Here, in the gloom of the cave, surrounded by the corpse-trophies of the nihtgenga, her silence was unnerving.

"Perhaps there is another way," said Bassus. "Maybe if we follow the beach southward, we might find an easier slope. Gram, go and see what you can find. Otherwise, we'll have to think how to get the girl up the cliff. This place is not safe."

Gram left the cave, but returned only moments later.

"You cannot have looked for another trail up to the clifftop in that time," said Bassus.

The back of Octa's neck prickled. Perhaps the beast had returned to its lair. But surely Gram would have raised the alarm with a shout.

"I have not looked," Gram said, "but I can tell you there is no way up for any of us until dawn now."

"How so?" replied Bassus. "It is not even dusk."

At that very instant, a wave crashed outside, the noise suddenly loud in the echoing chamber. Spray splashed the walls of the entrance and water lapped the rocks there.

"True," said Gram, his expression sombre, "but it will be dark soon and it seems the night has brought the tide. I fear we will need to sleep once more in dismal surroundings."

Octa sighed. The thought of spending a night in this gore-strewn cavern filled him with dread.

"And," Octa said, running his left hand over his stubbled jaw, "pray that the shadow-stalker cannot swim."

Fifteen

"Perhaps the creature has crawled into a hole somewhere and died," said Gram. "He took a mighty blow from you, Bassus. And you, Octa."

Octa remembered the jolt of pain in his wrist as he hammered Hrunting's blade into the monster's side. It had been like hitting the rocks of the cliff. He could not believe that the beast would have simply curled up and succumbed to its wounds.

"Perhaps," said Bassus, but he did not sound convinced. His eyes were shadowed with dark rings, as if bruised. He was exhausted. They all were, bones and muscles leaden. In those few moments when they had been able to close their eyes, they had slept fitfully at best. They had each taken a watch, expecting the huge bulk of the night-walker to suddenly burst through the mouth of the cavern.

Octa had stirred the embers and breathed fresh life into the fire, feeding it all the slivers of wood and twigs he could find on the sandy floor. Once the flames were flickering, the girl silently approached with large pieces of driftwood that had been stored at the back of the cave. Octa nodded his thanks, but Wealhtheow did not speak, instead returning to her nest in the animal skins. From there she watched, her gleaming eyes missing nothing.

The driftwood, worn smooth by the constant motion of the sea, burnt with strange hues of green and blue. Perhaps the wood was magic, or cursed, shot through with elf barbs. But it had given them enough heat and light to see them through till pale fingers of grey dawn light scratched the darkness away from the cave.

Outside, the day was chill and calm. The tide had receded and the waves rolled gently up the sand and pebbles of the beach. All the world was once more clad in a shroud of mist. Hidden now were the distant islands, and when they looked up the cliff, they could not discern the top.

"Unferth!" Bassus bellowed into the fog, making Octa start. Beside him, Wealhtheow, fragile and pale as a dove in her nightclothes of linen, pulled the bearskin tighter about her shoulders. She had still not spoken, but had followed them out of the cavern and into the misty morning.

"Unferth!" yelled Bassus again. There was no reply. Gram looked at Octa. Had the old man fled, that look said. Or perhaps something worse had befallen him.

And then, as thin as Hrothgar's ale, came a reply from high above them on the clouded clifftop.

"I am here, Bassus," Unferth shouted. "I thought you all dead."

"We all yet live," called Bassus. "And we have found Hrothgar's daughter. She is alive and seems well enough."

"And the beast?" called Unferth.

"No sign."

"Come up then," yelled Unferth. "I am cold and have seen no living thing this past night."

"I wonder where the beast is," Octa voiced the question they all pondered.

"I know not," answered Bassus, "but we cannot stay here. We must get the lass back to her folk. Then we can find a rope and return for the creature. I'll not be trapped down here when the tide returns."

Octa shivered.

"Can you climb?" Bassus asked Wealhtheow, a tenderness entering his tone.

Without looking up at the rocky cliff-face, she nodded.

"Good. Octa, lead the way. I will follow. Then you," Bassus indicated the girl. "Gram, you will come last and help Wealhtheow, if she needs it."

Octa was not keen on climbing the cliff again, but there was no other way up from the beach. He swung his arms a couple of times to free the muscles, and tucked his cloak into his belt to prevent it flapping.

"We're coming up," Octa shouted into the mist. Unferth evidently did not think a reply was necessary.

Octa spat into the sand and gripped the rocks.

The climb up was less arduous than the descent. It was not easy, but there was no biting breeze threatening to dislodge him. Searching for handholds and ledges above was simpler too, with less straining to see where he could place his feet. And he even found that he remembered some of the cracks and outcrops that had helped him the day before.

The birds too, seemed to have decided that they would let the climbers ascend unmolested. Perhaps it was because of the fog, but none of the white gulls came wheeling in about them now. Instead the warriors and the girl climbed in silence into the murk of the mists.

Despite the improvement over the previous day, the climb was still tough. Octa was less than halfway up before his arms and fingers were burning from the exertion. His breath billowed in steamy clouds around his head. Looking down he saw Bassus, red-faced and panting, a short distance below. The beach was still visible, but hazy. The clifftop was yet smothered in mist.

He continued up, his breath ragged now in his throat. Sweat plastered his fair hair to his forehead.

How much further? The fog was thicker now it seemed. Peering down he could just make out Bassus, but Gram and the girl were hidden from view. Above, the rock rose in a craggy wall to disappear into the gloom. He reached for a white-streaked crevice. Checking his grip was strong, he heaved himself up, until he was able to place his foot on a small jutting step of stone. He rested for a moment, taking deep breaths of the cold, moist morning air.

He peered into the mists above. Still no sign of the end of the cliff. It was as if he climbed in a magical realm, a land where there was no limit to this cliff. Perhaps the gods were gazing down, laughing at the foolish men, knowing that they would never reach the summit.

Octa shook his head to clear it of such thoughts. Beneath him, Bassus laboured, puffing as he pulled his bulk up. The sound of the waves rolling on the beach and sighing away again was clear and loud. This was nothing more than a cliff on a misty winter's day. Nothing more.

He turned his attention once more to the climb, he must be well over halfway by now.

"Unferth?" he called, hoping to get an idea of the man's distance from his reply.

Instead, there came an ululating howl, followed by a crash. The sound of shields colliding. Or of something large and heavy striking a shield.

The noise was close.

"Unferth!" he called again, but no reply came. The sounds of a struggle continued. A grunt. The bone-crunching clash of linden-board again. A scream.

There was nothing Octa could do here, hanging from the cliff. He gritted his teeth and clambered up as fast as he was able.

Sixteen

The last stretch of cliff seemed interminable, but surely only measured twice the height of a man. All the while Octa could hear the sounds of battle. At moments the grunts and clamour of conflict grew louder, then subsided, as if the mists played tricks with his ears. Octa did not speak further. Perhaps the beast had not heard his calls, for surely it must be the nihtgenga returned to its lair who now fought Unferth.

After what felt like an age, Octa's hand grasped the spiny branches of a sea buckthorn. He pulled himself the rest of the way over the top of the cliff, sure that at any moment, the beast would spy him and send him tumbling to his death on the rocks below. But no attack came. Unferth had occupied the creature's attention, but was sorely pressed.

The old thegn was standing, crouched, shield poised in defence. As Octa watched, the huge beast, all lumbering shaggy fur, rushed forward with terrible speed. Unferth jabbed at the monster with his spear. It retreated. Unferth had done well to keep it at bay this long, alone as he had been. But he was alone no longer. Octa stepped away from the edge of the cliff and dragged Hrunting from its scabbard. The blade thrummed, as if with pent-up sword song.

"By order of Edwin King, your life is forfeit, beast," he said, unknowing whether the thing understood the words. "You have killed for the last time. Now you die."

The giant swung its head towards Octa, its mane of fur quivering. For an instant, the thing stood there, gazing its black hatred at the fair youthful warrior who stood now before it. Octa willed Unferth to seize the opportunity that had presented itself. With no defences to contend with, Unferth could plunge his spear deep into the beast. Octa held the dark stare of the creature.

Go on, by Woden, kill it!

But Unferth did not attack. The old warrior, face pale and terrified, saw a different chance – to escape. He turned quickly and fled. In a moment, he was lost in the mists.

The beast did not even look at the fleeing thegn. It lifted its head to the sky and let out the drawn-out howl Octa had heard on the climb. Its breath billowed above it into the fog. And then, dropping its head like a boar that has been cornered by hounds, the nihtgenga charged towards Octa.

He barely had time to react, such was the creature's speed. He swung his sword at the fell beast, but as before, his blow clattered from its body as if it were made of stone. An instant later, it collided with him, sending him reeling to the earth.

Octa felt a stabbing pain in his left arm. He rolled away and leapt back up to his feet. Where was the edge of the cliff? A quick glance revealed he was but a few paces from plunging to his doom. His arm throbbed. Blood seeped through the sleeve of his kirtle. The creature had cut him. Had it bitten him? But there was no time to think, again it rushed at him. Octa brought Hrunting up and aimed a savage cut to the creature's chest. It made no effort to avoid the blow, and the patterned blade smashed against it. The sword did not penetrate flesh, but deflected with a clang. Octa was ready this time. He did not allow himself to be thrown to the ground. He leapt away from the monster's attack.

There was a gleam of metal there. What was that?

The monster took a pace backward, perhaps wary of Hrunting's flashing blade.

For a heartbeat they stood staring at each other; the dark, fur-covered beast and the golden-haired warrior. Octa surveyed his adversary. The fog was thick, but there was enough light to make out details he had not seen before. Octa shifted his footing, edging away from the deadly fall of the cliff.

The beast's head was like that of a boar; wiry hair, and tusks protruding from a gaping maw. Octa shuddered. The creature's huge bulk was covered in thick, matted fur. Again that glint of metal. And Octa's eyes widened in surprise.

The monster, perhaps reacting to Octa's sudden realisation, leapt forward with a howling scream of inchoate rage.

Octa's mind was a-spin, but he knew now what he must do. He allowed the creature to speed towards him and at the very last moment, he sidestepped and struck downward with his sword. He felt the blade strike and bite, deep into soft, pliant flesh. The shadow-walker screamed; a very human sound.

It spun around to face Octa once more. Hot breath clouded about its snout. The night-stalker was not now protected by darkness. And as the thin winter sun filtered through the mists to illuminate the creature, Octa was suddenly certain of what he had suspected moments before.

This was no monster.

It was a man. A huge man, with eyes full of madness and skin smothered in mire and old gore. Perhaps more animal than man in his thoughts, but a man nonetheless. His head was wreathed in a boar's skull and his shoulders and arms were encased in a matted bear pelt. Octa could see now that the man's hands were black with grime and death, but they were the hands of a man. In each massive hand he gripped a savage-looking seax. The blades did not glimmer and shine as fine iron should. It looked as though they had never been cleaned, but Octa could feel his warm blood running down his left arm – those seaxes were sharp enough.

Beneath the bear skin, the gleam that Octa had seen was a byrnie of iron links. The creature did not have stone-like skin. Where the bear's fur ended, fresh blood oozed down the man's left leg. Octa took in all of this in a heartbeat.

"Your slaughter-dew is as red as anyone's," he said. "You have killed your last. Today, your blood will soak the land. The wolves and ravens will pick your bones before this day is through."

The beast-man did not reply, he merely bellowed and ran at Octa, vicious seax blades slicing the air.

Such speed for one so huge! Just in time, Octa lifted Hrunting, but his enemy came on so fast he was unable to place his blow as he wanted. Instead he jabbed the blade forward in a frantic attempt to pierce the man's iron-knit shirt. Hrunting's point glanced across the rings and buried the full length of the blade through the thick bear pelt. The sword was trapped. Useless.

Octa let go of Hrunting's hilt and grasped the man's wrists. The night-walker crashed into him and they fell to the damp grass. Octa could not breathe, the air had been knocked from his lungs and now the huge man straddled him, his weight pressing onto Octa's chest. Octa gripped the wrists and pushed with all his might, but he knew those wicked blades would find their mark. The man was too strong, too heavy.

The beast's eyes flared wide in savage glee as he sensed victory. The seaxes moved inexorably towards Octa's exposed throat. Panic rose up in Octa like bile, acid and burning. And then the man-beast laughed, that rock-crunching chuckle that had filled them with fear when they had been lost in the marsh. Octa saw the man's teeth, like blood-stained grave markers in his gaping maw. His foetid breath washed over him, a miasma of murder and man-flesh.

Octa could feel his grip weakening. The blood-smeared blades touched his neck. Octa heaved, but he could not push the seaxes away. He would die here. If only he could draw breath, perhaps he would find the strength he needed.

Death's cold fingers scratched his neck.

His vision blurred.

And then, the man-monster was gone. In a screaming clash of bodies, it was thrown from atop Octa.

Octa lay there blinking, gulping in great lungfuls of moist, cold air. What had happened?

Then the sounds came rushing in on him like a storm-blown sea crashing into a cliff.

Someone was screaming.

Bassus.

He must help his friend. Octa rolled over and pushed himself up. His head felt as though it were not part of him, but he managed to stagger to his feet. Where was his sword? It was nowhere near him.

A few paces away, Bassus now faced the night-stalker. He sent a blow towards the creature's eyes. A feint, that then slid into an attack on its chest. The blade rattled over the hidden byrnie, and the beast dropped its shoulder and barged into the thegn. Bassus sprawled to the earth.

"No!" Octa shouted, finding his voice. "It wears a byrnie. That is why we cannot cut it. It is no monster. Just a man. He bleeds. He will die."

The man turned to Octa once more and rushed towards him without a moment's pause.

Octa did not even have time to draw his seax from its scabbard at his belt. He raised his hands in defence and again attempted to grasp the huge wrists. His right hand found its target, but his left missed and pain seared his side as the seax sliced across his ribs. The beast-man clattered into him. Octa absorbed some of the force of the impact taking rapid steps backward. He did not wish to find himself once more on the ground with this thing on his chest.

They staggered back for a heartbeat, grappling with each other like wrestlers after a feast. Then, with a terrible sinking feeling, Octa found there was no earth left behind him for his feet.

With no time to even let out a scream, both Octa and the beast tumbled over the cliff.

Seventeen

The world spun. Something hard cracked into Octa's jaw, rattling his teeth. Flailing, without thought, his hand lashed out and caught hold of the sea buckthorn. Some part of his mind, the part that was more beast than man, recalled the cliff-face that he had so recently scaled. With bone-jarring force, his chest smashed into the rocks of the cliff. His ribs, slick with blood now, were a screaming agony. Twigs, thorns and leaves ripped through his fingers, shredding the skin of his palm. A few berries that remained on the plant erupted with thick, oily juice that mingled with the blood from his broken skin.

And then, his fall halted. A surge of relief flooded through him. But the instant he began to believe he was safe, the truth of his plight came crashing down upon him. His hand could not hold him, weighted down as he was.

Twisting his head he saw that the night-walker, with his inhuman speed, had let go its blades and now clung to Octa's cloak. Octa was strong, but he could not hold such a bulk for long. He reached up with his left hand and clasped it around the thorny branches of the sea buckthorn. The spines dug deep into his flesh, but he scarcely noticed. Thus, with both hands tight about the plant, he heaved. But it was no use, he could not pull them both up. Pebbles and earth, loosened from around the base of the plant, showered into Octa's eyes. He blinked away the dirt, trying not to give in to the panic that threatened to engulf him.

The man-beast growled and began climbing up his back, hand over hand. Octa kicked out, in an attempt to dislodge the huge man. More dirt fell, and they both shifted downward, as the plant's roots began to lose their grip on the soil. Octa grunted as his ribs once more scraped against the rocks. The slash on his left arm throbbed in time to his pounding heart.

"By Woden," Octa hissed through gritted teeth, "you will not live to see another night."

The beast chuckled, dark and gurgling. It began pulling itself up to safety with its massive, grime-smeared hands.

Octa would not allow this foul thing to live. It had killed too many, brought so much fear to the land. Now, it must pay the price that all murderers must pay.

Letting go with his left hand, Octa hammered his elbow down and back. Hard. It connected with the man's neck. Octa's right hand was slipping. His kirtle was drenched in blood now, but the pain had ceased. He smashed his elbow down again and again. Blood splattered from his wounded arm over the upturned boar maw. The tusks dug into his flesh with each hit. Savagely pummelling into the beast-man's neck, head and shoulder, Octa did not allow the man to recover, following each blow with another. His right shoulder screamed in silent anguish and his fingers ripped through the remaining branches of the buckthorn. They would both surely fall.

But Octa did not stop. Someone was screaming, a guttural, throat-tearing sound. With a sense of wonder he realised it was his voice that rent the fog-cloaked air.

He continued hitting the man-slayer, until without warning, it released its right hand from his cloak. The nihtgenga's bulk shifted, and Octa was certain this was it, the moment his grip would give way and they would fall to where he could hear the roll and pull of the waves breaking on hidden rocks far below.

Looking down, he saw the man's eyes, red-rimmed and dark, blazing with a terrible ire. His left hand was wrapped tightly into the damp wool of Octa's cloak. His right hand now bunched into a fist, huge and gnarled. For a heartbeat, the man-thing stared into Octa's eyes and then, with a flicker of a smile on its blood-encrusted lips, it hammered the fist into Octa's back, between his shoulder blades.

It was like being hit by a falling tree. Once again, the wind rushed from his lungs. Spots of darkness mottled his vision. His grip loosened on the thorny shrub.

Those eyes. The thing was truly mad. Was it even a man after all? Perhaps Paulinus was right and this was the kin of Cain, a mythical monster from a long-lost time. The creature laughed its boulder-crumbling laugh once more. Octa knew he would not be able to hold on if it struck him again. His strength was gone. He could barely draw a breath. His shoulder and arm was a white-hot agony of exertion. The nihtgenga raised its great fist.

Octa closed his eyes. He was spent. He could hold on no longer.

But the blow did not come.

"Die, you foul thing. Die!" came Bassus' shout.

Octa opened his eyes to see the great thegn burst from the fog. In his hand flickered his fine patterned-blade. The sword sliced down in a vicious arc. There was the dull hacking sound of butchery and hot blood gushed over Octa's face and back.

Suddenly, the weight fell away from him. The mad man of the marsh, the nihtgenga, the shadow-stalker, dropped without a sound. The fog swallowed him in an instant.

Octa drew in a shuddering breath. His limbs were trembling.

"I don't think I can pull myself up," he said, his voice as tremulous as his arms.

Bassus quickly knelt and reached out his hand.

"I've got you."

Bassus pulled him up, and Octa fell to the moist earth, still struggling to breathe.

Something pressed into his back. He reached behind him only to recoil with a yelp of fear. His fingers had brushed the still-warm, hair-bristled and heavily-muscled arm of the beast. It remained, oozing thick blood, tangled in his cloak, where Bassus had severed it.

Eighteen

"It might have been strong as an ox and mad as an aurochs," Gram said, looking down at the severed arm, "but I'll wager even that nihtgenga cannot survive having its arm hewn from its shoulder and then falling onto the rocks down there."

Octa still trembled as Wealhtheow and Gram stepped out of the mists. He had begun to shiver uncontrollably. He pulled his cloak about him, but he could not stop shaking. His teeth chattered. He had sat up, but did not trust his legs to stand.

Wealhtheow looked down at the limb, her eyes huge and liquid. But she did not speak.

"Unferth?" asked Gram.

Bassus looked into the fog, westward, towards the marsh. He hawked and spat.

"Fled."

Gram did not seem surprised. He knelt beside Octa, and rummaged in the bag he carried.

"If we do not bind your wounds, you'll be joining that beast in death soon enough. You are as pale and weak as a newborn lamb."

He produced a kirtle from his bag, and tore the cloth with his knife.

Octa's mind was swimming. He looked beyond Gram, into the swirling mists. He must be dreaming. He remembered having a fever as a child and seeing things that his mother later told him were not there. He had seen shadowy creatures then, standing at the end of his cot, red eyes boring into him where he had lain, drenched in sweat, trembling and mewling in terror.

"There is nothing there, my son," his mother had said, but he had never fully believed her. He knew what he had seen.

And now again he saw a shadow form in the mist. Stunted and hunched, it came towards them, gaining solidity and form as it approached. It scooped up Unferth's fallen spear from the grass and then Octa saw the truth of it. This was no shadow-creature, looming over a feverish child, it was Modthrith.

Hrothgar's wife rushed forward, feet silent on the soft earth. Octa wanted to shout out a warning, but his tongue was cleaved to his palate. She ran towards Bassus, a savage anger burning in those eyes. A crazed ire that Octa recognised.

Wealhtheow shattered the silence with a scream.

"No, mother!"

Bassus spun around. The spear-tip glinted in the pale light of the watery sun.

"My son!" shrieked Modthrith. "You have slain my beautiful son."

The spear streaked towards Bassus' heart, but with a warrior's grace, he twisted his body, allowing the point to pass by harmlessly. Catching the spear haft in his grip, he heaved, using Modthrith's own speed against her. Before she could react, Bassus had propelled her forward, away from him and over the edge of the cliff. She lost her grip on the spear and for the briefest of moments she seemed to hang there in the mists. And then she was gone with a wailing howl of anger and loss. A heartbeat later, her scream was silenced.

Wealhtheow stepped to the edge of the cliff and stared down into the murk.

"Poor mother," she said.

Turning, she went to the gnarled arm that lay on the earth. She reached out a tiny hand and stroked the hand. A tear trickled down her pallid cheek.

"Poor Grendel."

Nineteen

Octa allowed the warmth from the great hearth fire to soak into his bones. He normally preferred to sit further from the hearth when the fire was stoked high and blazing, but a chill had settled upon him on the journey back to Gefrin. By the time they had arrived he had been shaking uncontrollably. He had feared he would never get warm.

But he had stopped trembling. The good mead in his drinking horn and the thick, tasty stew in his belly seemed to be doing as much as the fire to warm him. Elda once more poured mead into his horn, offering him a coy smile. He hardly noticed. His head was full of recent memories which would not let him free of their grip.

He stretched the muscles of his back and grunted, regretting the movement. The blow from the nihtgenga had left a huge bruise, and the binding about his ribs did nothing to ease the burning pain from the cut he had received. His hands were also bound with strips of clean linen. The thorns of the sea buckthorn had left his palms torn and raw. Taking another sip of the sweet mead, he stared into the flames. They danced and spat sparks up into the air. Closing his eyes, he could see again Hrothgar's steading ablaze, smoke billowing into the darkening sky.

"You think we'll ever see Hrothgar and his other sons again?"

Octa opened his eyes and looked at Bassus. The older thegn was also subdued, quieter than normal. The events of the past few days had taken their toll on them all.

"I pray that we do not," said Octa. "I would forget Hrothgar and his kin, if I could."

Bassus nodded and took a long draught from his cup.

After Gram had bound Octa's wounds, they had set out for Hrothgar's home in the swamp. As the mists had lifted, they had seen a dark column of smoke. Following the smoke like a beacon, they had found all the buildings burning. There had been no sign of Hrothgar and his sons. Octa had been surprised that the man had heeded Bassus' warning about the king's horses. They were tethered close by, but far enough away from the flames for safety. The animals had rolled their eyes in fear at the conflagration, and seemed content enough to be gone from the place as they rode away from the marsh.

Wealhtheow had gazed silently at her old home, as the sod-covered roof collapsed in an explosion of sparks and roiling smoke. She had not uttered another word since the clifftop. Octa looked over at where she sat at the edge of the great hall. She was sat as she had been when they had found her in the cave, knees drawn up to her chest, dark eyes watching everything. She met his stare and he suppressed a shudder.

Without bidding, his eyes flicked to the grisly trophy that commanded attention in the hall. Grendel's arm, muscled and mottled, pale in death, yet still exuding the power of the man-beast, hung, hand down from where it had been nailed to a beam.

Edwin had been overjoyed that they had returned with a token to show that the night-walker was dead.

"You have slain the great beast," he had said, his voice full of praise. "Do I not have the doughtiest of gesithas?" he had asked of the inhabitants of the hall. The gathered men and women cheered their king and his warriors. The darkness of the winter nights was a little safer now.

"It was not a beast, my lord king," Bassus had said, striding forth with the arm. "It was but a man. Moonstruck and evil, but a man nonetheless."

The hall had grown silent.

Edwin had frowned.

"Indeed? But where is Wiglaf the quick, and what of brave Unferth? Were they slain by a mere man?"

Octa had recalled Grendel's power, the huge bulk beneath the matted furs and iron shirt. The blazing madness in his eyes. Was he truly just a man?

"Alas, Wiglaf fell," said Bassus.

"And Unferth, most trusted of thegns? What of Unferth?" The king's brows furrowed.

Bassus took in a deep breath and proffered Hrunting to his king. "He too was lost," he said, at last.

Octa had wondered at Bassus' words, but then nodded to himself. Why speak of Unferth's cowardice? Why bring shame upon him? If he yet lived, he would never return to Edwin's hall. He was a thegn who had abandoned his

88

spear-brothers. One so craven would never show his face again.

Edwin had looked upon the fine blade, his face a mask of sadness. At long last, he drew himself up to his full height.

"You have done a great service to me and the people of Bernicia. I can see that you have suffered much on your quest to rid us of the nihtgenga. So, rest now, fill your bellies with hot food. Slake your thirst on my finest mead. You will be well rewarded for killing this monster, but for now, recover your strength. Feast and be merry. For no longer should we be fearful of the winter's nights. The fell beast is dead."

He had lifted up the pallid arm and the hall had erupted with a roar of approval.

Now, with his shaking finally subsided, Octa felt a tide of exhaustion wash over him. He needed sleep. He hoped he would not dream of the mad eyes and the great weight pulling him down, the sea buckthorn ripping through his fingers.

But first he needed a piss. Pushing himself to his feet with a wince at the pain in his arm, ribs and back, he walked stiffly to the door of the hall. A small figure ran up beside him as he left the warmth and stepped into the frigid air of the Northumbrian night. It was Ælfhere, the scop. The man's eyes twinkled with excitement like the stars that shone in the cloudless sky above the hills surrounding Gefrin.

Ælfhere fell into step beside Octa.

"Mind if I join you?" Ælfhere said.

Octa was in no mood for pleasantries.

"Do what you want, scop." His breath clouded before him. "If you need to piss, you need to piss. It is no concern of mine."

Ælfhere laughed. Octa frowned. The man spun a good yarn and was a talented tale-teller, but his frivolity often rankled with Octa.

"The beast's name was Grendel, you say?" Ælfhere asked.

"I did not say, but yes. Grendel is what Wealhtheow called him."

"Wealhtheow, yes." Ælfhere was slightly breathless, having to almost run to keep up with Octa's long strides. "Interesting names. Fine names."

Octa ignored him and walked on in silence.

Ælfhere trotted along beside him, seemingly unable to stop talking.

"And the father of the beast was Hrothgar?"

"It was no beast, merely a man."

"Yes, yes. But in the tale, it will be a beast. A great monster. A giant. Kin of Cain, was that not what that Christ priest called it?"

They had walked far enough. Octa halted and loosened his breeches. With a sigh of satisfaction, he released the pressure from his bladder. Steam rose from the frosted grass. He noted that Ælfhere did not join him. So he had no need to relieve himself.

"You mean to tell the tale of this night-stalker?" Octa asked, fastening his breeches.

"Of course. I have long been dreaming up a great saga. A story of distant lands. Of Svears and Geats. Wyrms and monsters. But it needed something else."

"And this Grendel is what you needed?" Octa spat and turned to walk back to the hall. The noise of laughter and chatter came to them on the still, cold air.

"Oh yes," Ælfhere's eyes glittered. "I can see the tale forming in my mind. The monster, kin of Cain, attacking the king and his host in their great hall."

"But that is not what happened," replied Octa. He had no time for this wittering bard. He made to step past him, but Ælfhere blocked his path.

"This will be greater than what happened. All the best tales are." He laughed again. "I am still searching for a name for the hero of the tale. A tall, fair warrior who slays the beast and frees the kingdom." Ælfhere looked Octa up and down appraisingly.

"Not I. I do not want to be remembered for killing a mad man and his mother." And then a thought struck him. All he wished was to be free of this annoying man, to be able to return to the hall and find somewhere to sleep. He imagined his brother, back in Cantware, so keen to be a warrior. He too was tall, fair and strong. And wouldn't he love to be the hero of a scop's tale?

"How about Beobrand?" he said.

"For the hero? Hmmm..." Ælfhere scratched his beard and tilted his head, as if listening to the sound of the name. "Beobrand. Beobrand. No, it is not quite right. Beo... Beo..."

Far off, in the hills overlooking the settlement a wolf howled, its long, plaintive call reminding them that the night was still not safe from all danger.

For a moment, both men stood listening to the echo of the wolf's moaning voice.

"Hmmm... a wolf," said Ælfhere. "Yes, that might just work."

Octa looked down at the scop. The small man was practically jumping from one foot to the other, such was his delight.

"What?" asked Octa, finding himself being drawn into Ælfhere's enthusiasm, despite himself. "What might work?"

"The hero's name," Ælfhere answered, his tone gleeful. "I have it. The hero shall be called... Beowulf!"

Author's Note

The exact date of the composition of the epic poem, "Beowulf", is unknown. Hygelac, Beowulf's first lord was, as were several other characters in the poem, a real person who is recorded in the Frankish annals as having died in AD 521. The only manuscript of the poem to have survived to the present day dates from around AD 1000. It is in the Nowell Codex, which is now located in the British Library. The poem, that is widely regarded as one of the most important pieces of Old English literature, was very nearly lost back in 1731. It was badly damaged by a fire that swept through Ashburnham House in London where it was in a collection of medieval manuscripts assembled by Sir Robert Bruce Cotton.

Though there is disagreement on the date of composition of the poem, most scholars agree that it was passed down for generations as part of the rich oral tradition of the Anglo-Saxons.

The events of the poem do not actually take place in Britain, though it is written in Old English. Rather it hearkens back to the distant past and the lands of the forebears of the Germanic tribes that settled in the British Isles. The story takes place in Denmark and Sweden. The saga is fabulous, full of strong imagery of mead halls, warriors, ring-giving lords, and of course, monsters. It has been the inspiration for countless works of fiction, from Tolkien's *Lord of the Rings*, to recent movies and television series that have attempted to bring the magnificent story to life.

The seed of my retelling of part of Beowulf's story, or more accurately, my tale of incidents that could have inspired some of Beowulf's story, came when a reader who had read *The Serpent Sword* contacted me and asked the question, "Is the sword in the novel *the* Hrunting?" Now, the truth of the matter was that I had wanted to use a real name for the famed sword in my novel and found such names were few. There are others, and it was also tempting to create a name for the sword, but in the end, I picked the name of one of the swords from Beowulf, liking the hint at the mythology of the blade, and the fact that it does not always serve its master well.

But the question played on my mind. What if, I asked myself, it was *the* Hrunting? What if the sword was part of the inspiration for the poem of Beowulf? Perhaps the poem had been composed in Britain by a scop seeking to remind his people of their illustrious past. Could there be a way for me to tell the story without having to fall into the realms of fantasy, of dragons and ogres?

I went on to write the third novel in the Bernicia Chronicles, *Blood and Blade*, but all the while, in the back of my mind the seeds of the tale that would become *Kin of Cain* were germinating.

This novella is a fanciful imagining of events that could have perhaps sparked the muse in a fellow storyteller well over a thousand years ago. The people of the seventh century believed in monsters that stalked the night and prowled the lonely places of the wilds, the fens and the moors, so I do not think it is unlikely that if animals and people were killed in savage attacks with no witnesses, the murders would have been attributed to all sorts of dire and magical creatures. After all, think of the hysteria that gripped London during the Whitechapel murders of the nineteenth century and of the various outlandish identities people dreamt up for the elusive Jack the Ripper.

It doesn't take a huge leap to imagine something like this occurring back in the sparsely populated countryside of Northumbria where perhaps, just perhaps, a poet might have been mulling over ideas for a saga about a warrior of renown who would become a great king. A man who would kill monsters and dragons and lead his people with honour. Perhaps the story and the character of "Beowulf" were not just figments of a bard's imagination, maybe there really was a warrior who, back in the darkest reaches of the past, fought, and killed, the Kin of Cain.

Acknowledgements

As always, thanks must go first and foremost to you, dear reader, for picking up this book and reading it. I hope you have enjoyed it. If you have, please tell others about it, and if you want to be exceptionally nice, leave a short review on the online retailer of your choice. Reviews and ratings really help new readers to make a decision on whether to spend hours of their life reading a book, so online reviews truly make a difference.

I must also thank James Webb, for asking me the question about Hrunting that sparked my imagination.

As usual, I gave the book to several test readers, so thanks to Gareth Jones, Graham Glendinning, Richard Ward, Shane Smart, Emmett Carter, Alex Forbes and Simon Blunsdon for reading early drafts and providing feedback. Their comments were, as ever, extremely useful in helping to polish the final version.

I would like to thank my agent, Robin Wade, for his unwavering support and no-nonsense approach to publishing.

Everyone in the Aria/Head of Zeus family has been great and I love being part of such a dedicated and talented team. Special thanks to Caroline Ridding, Nia Beynon, Yasemin Turan and Paul King.

There are too many to mention here by name, but I must thank all the historical fiction authors and readers who always provide such great support online. The whole process of writing would be a lot more isolated and difficult without the camaraderie of so many friends from the huge virtual world of the Internet.

And lastly, extra special thanks to my family, Elora, Iona and Maite, for all their love, encouragement and support and, of course, for putting up with me.

About Matthew Harffy

MATTHEW HARFFY has worked in the IT industry, where he spent all day writing and editing, just not the words that most interested him. Prior to that he worked in Spain as an English teacher and translator. Matthew lives in Wiltshire, England, with his wife and their two daughters. When not writing or spending time with his family, Matthew sings in a band called Rock Dog.

Hello from Aria

We hope you enjoyed this book! Let us know, we'd love to hear from you.

We are Aria, a dynamic digital-first fiction imprint from award-winning independent publishers Head of Zeus. At heart, we're avid readers committed to publishing exactly the kind of books we love to read – from romance and sagas to crime, thrillers and historical adventures. Visit us online and discover a community of like-minded fiction fans!

We're also on the look out for tomorrow's superstar authors. So, if you're a budding writer looking for a publisher, we'd love to hear from you. You can submit your book online at ariafiction.com/ we-want-read-your-book

You can find us at:
Email: aria@headofzeus.com
Website: www.ariafiction.com
Submissions: www.ariafiction.com/ we-want-read-your-book
Facebook: @ariafiction
Twitter: @Aria_Fiction
Instagram: @ariafiction

Printed in Great Britain
by Amazon

72445806R00068